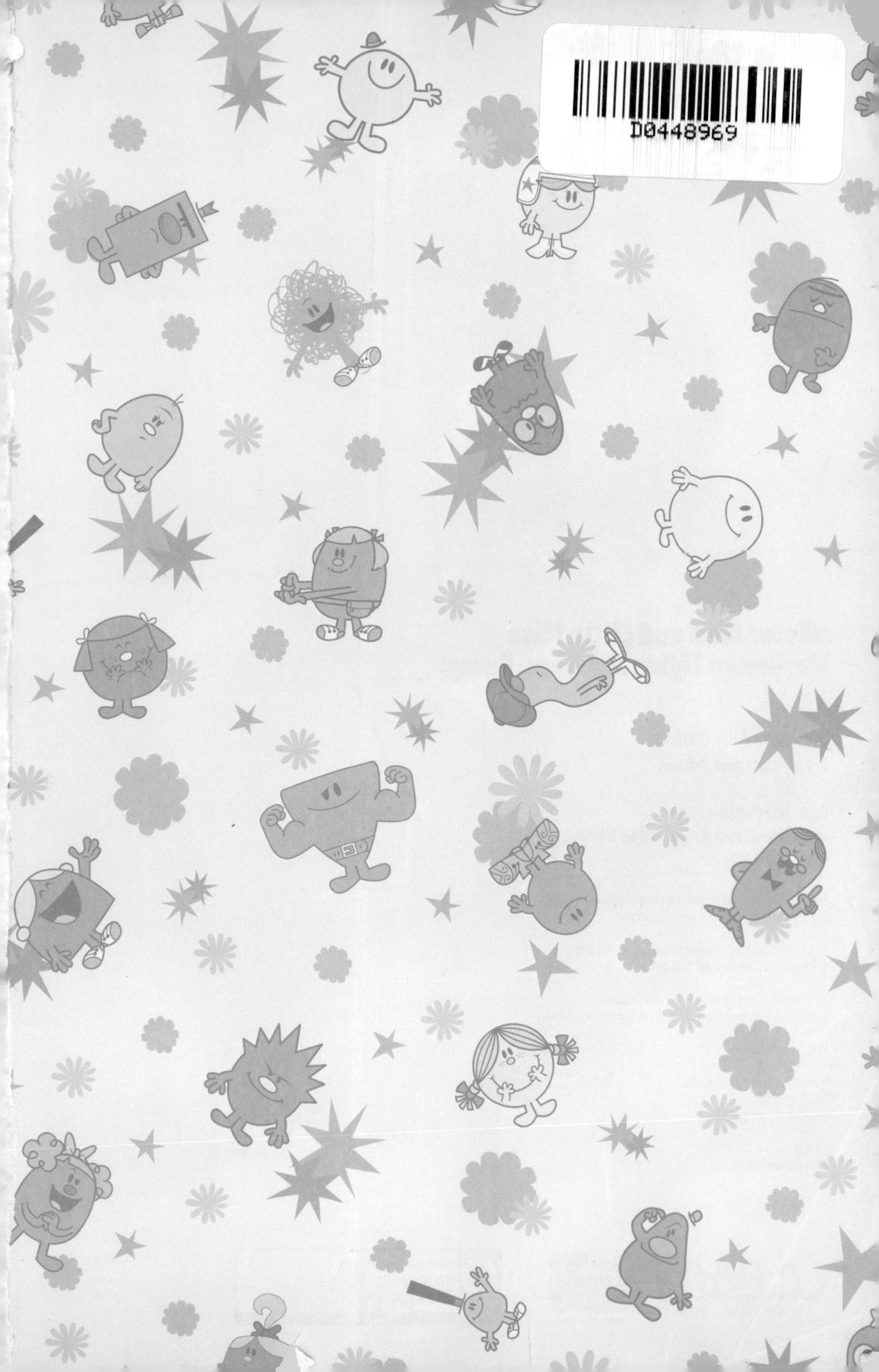

Mister Men and Little Miss
Mr. Bump: Lights, Camera, Bump!

Stories by John Hardman
Art by Matthew Britton

Cover Art • Matthew Britton
Graphics and Cover Design • Yukiko Whitley
Editor • Traci N. Todd

Printed in China

Published by VIZ Media, LLC
P.O. Box 77010
San Francisco, CA 94107

10 9 8 7 6 5 4 3 2 1
First printing, April 2012

vizkids
www.vizkids.com

VIZ media
www.viz.com

RATED A FOR ALL AGES

PARENTAL ADVISORY
MR. MEN AND LITTLE MISS
MR. BUMP: LIGHTS CAMERA BUMP! is rated
A and is suitable for readers of all ages.

ratings.viz.com

MR. MEN LITTLE MISS™

Mr. Bump

Lights, Camera, Bump!

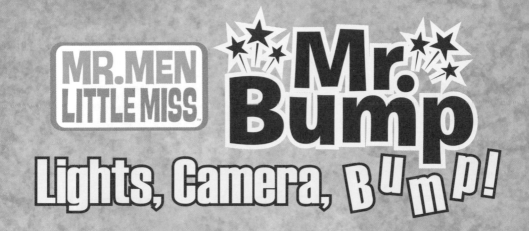

Meet the Mr. Men and Little Misses!

Little Miss Sunshine

Mr. Happy

Mr. Bump

Little Miss Daredevil

Mr. Grumpy

Mr. Strong

Mr. Lazy

Little Miss Scary

Mr. Scatterbrain

Mr. Tall

Mr. Messy

Mr. Nosy

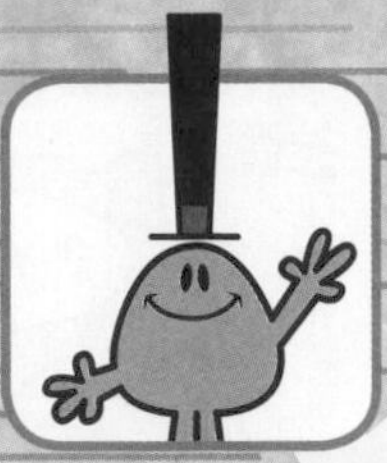
Mr. Small

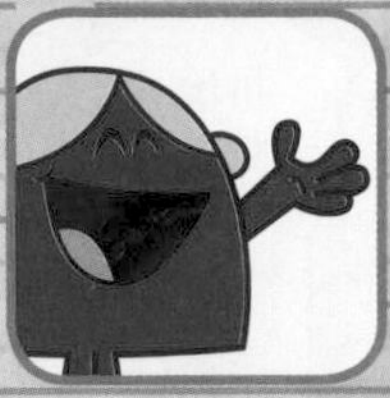
Little Miss Chatterbox

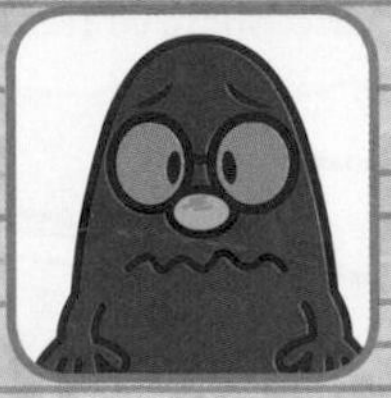
Mr. Nervous

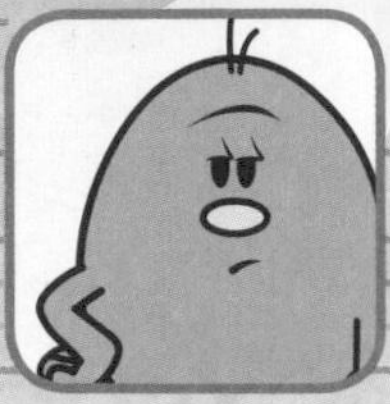
Mr. Quiet

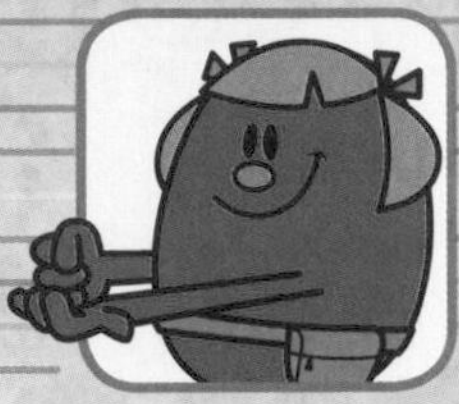
Little Miss Helpful

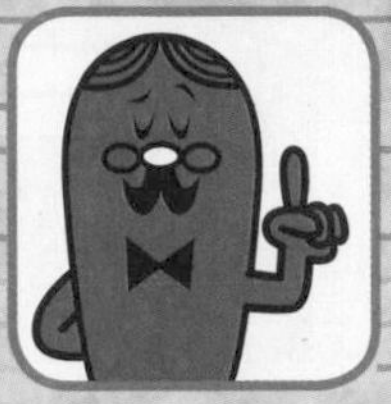
Mr. Fussy

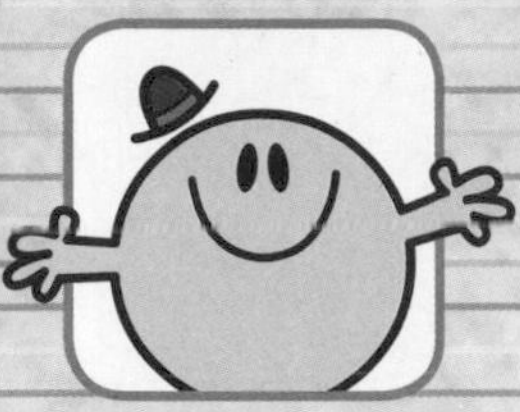
Mr. Bounce

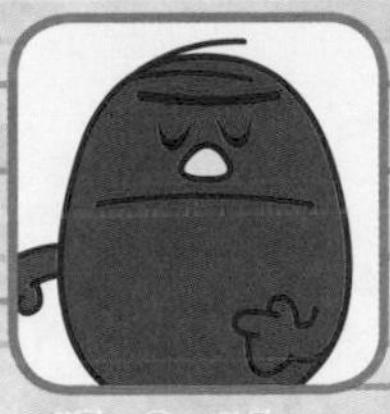
Mr. Stubborn

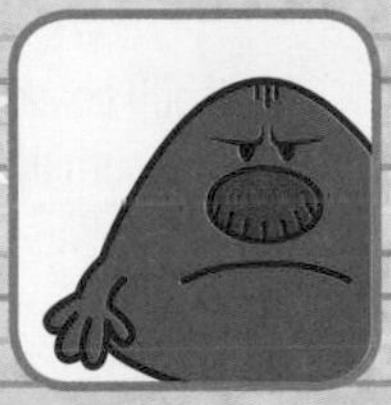
Mr. Rude

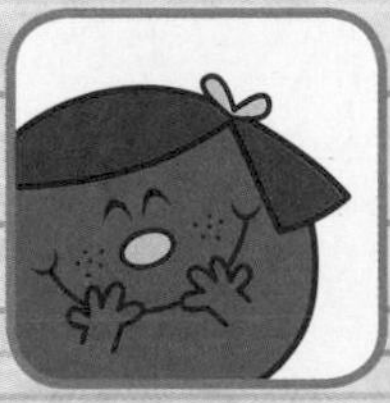
Little Miss Giggles

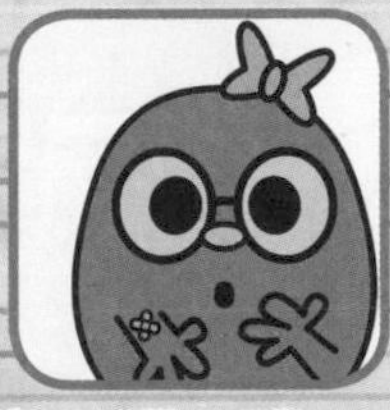
Little Miss Whoops

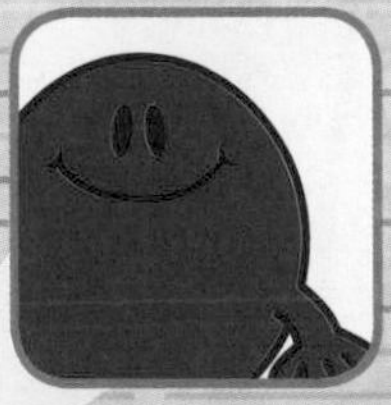
Mr. Noisy

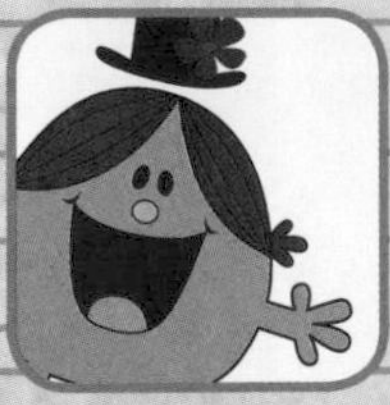
Little Miss Magic

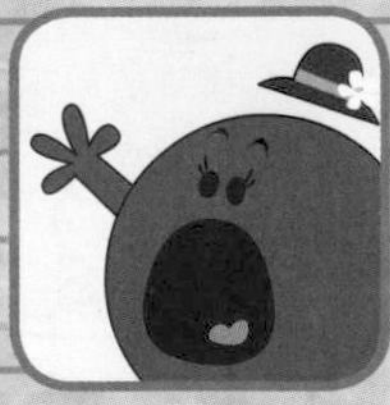
Little Miss Bossy

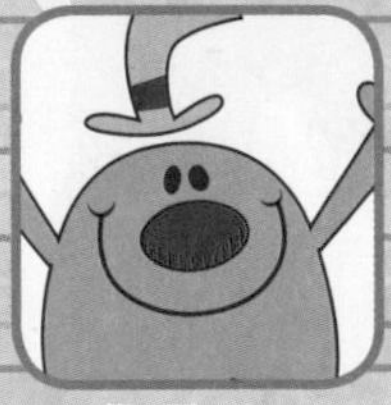
Mr. Funny

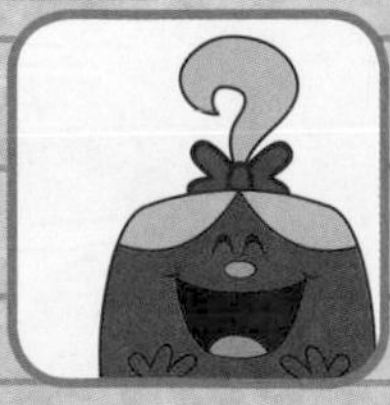
Little Miss Curious

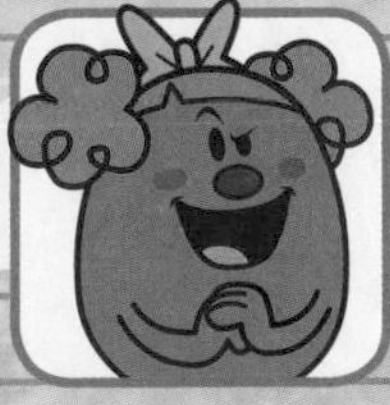
Little Miss Naughty

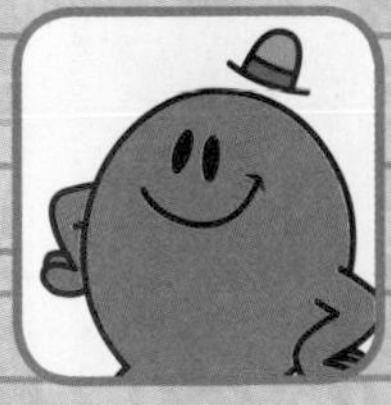
Mr. Tickle

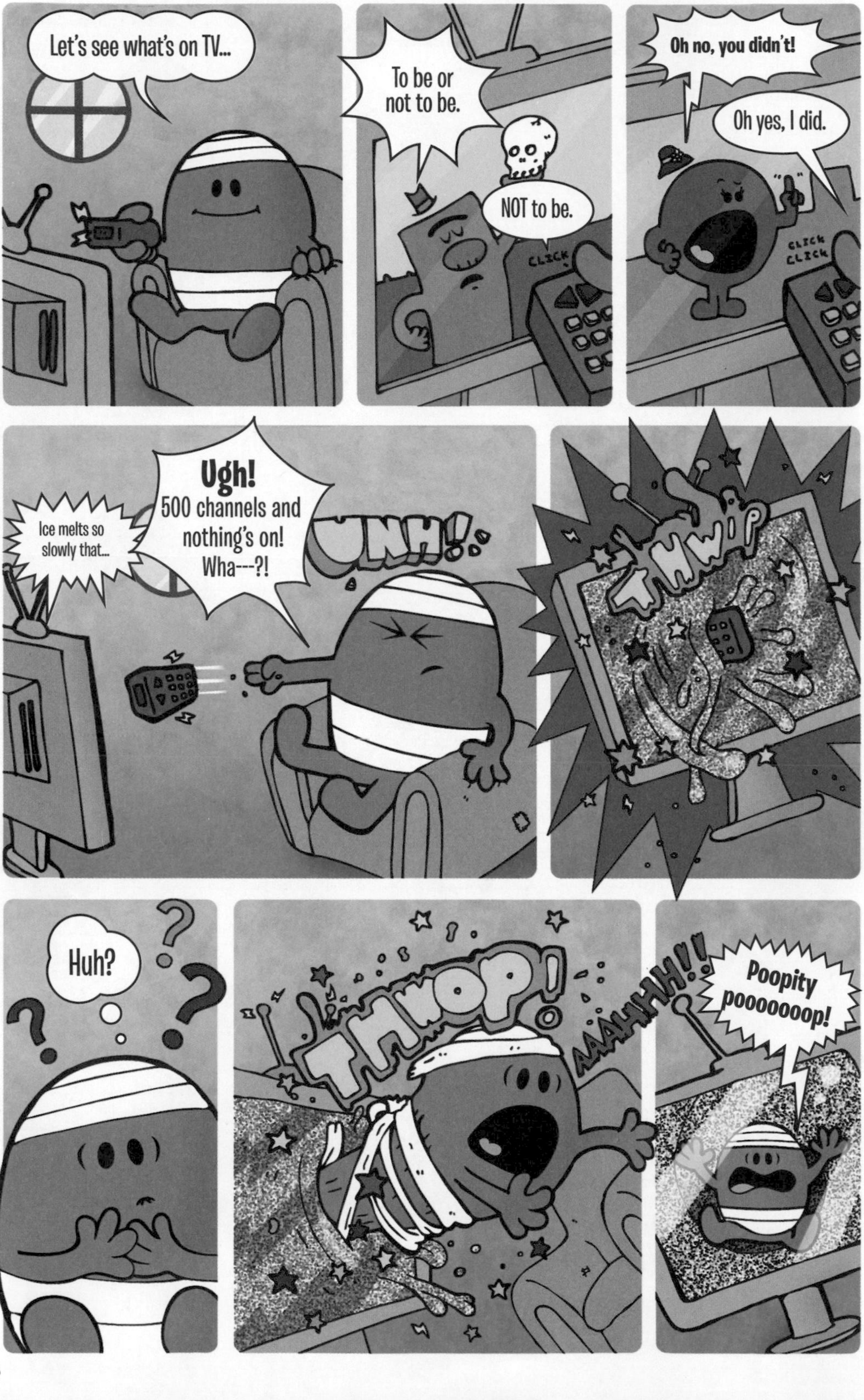

Let's see what's on TV...
To be or not to be.
NOT to be.
CLICK
Oh no, you didn't!
Oh yes, I did.
CLICK CLICK
Ice melts so slowly that...
Ugh! 500 channels and nothing's on! Wha---?!
UNH!!
THWIP
Huh?
THWOP!
AAAHHH!!
Poopity pooooooop!

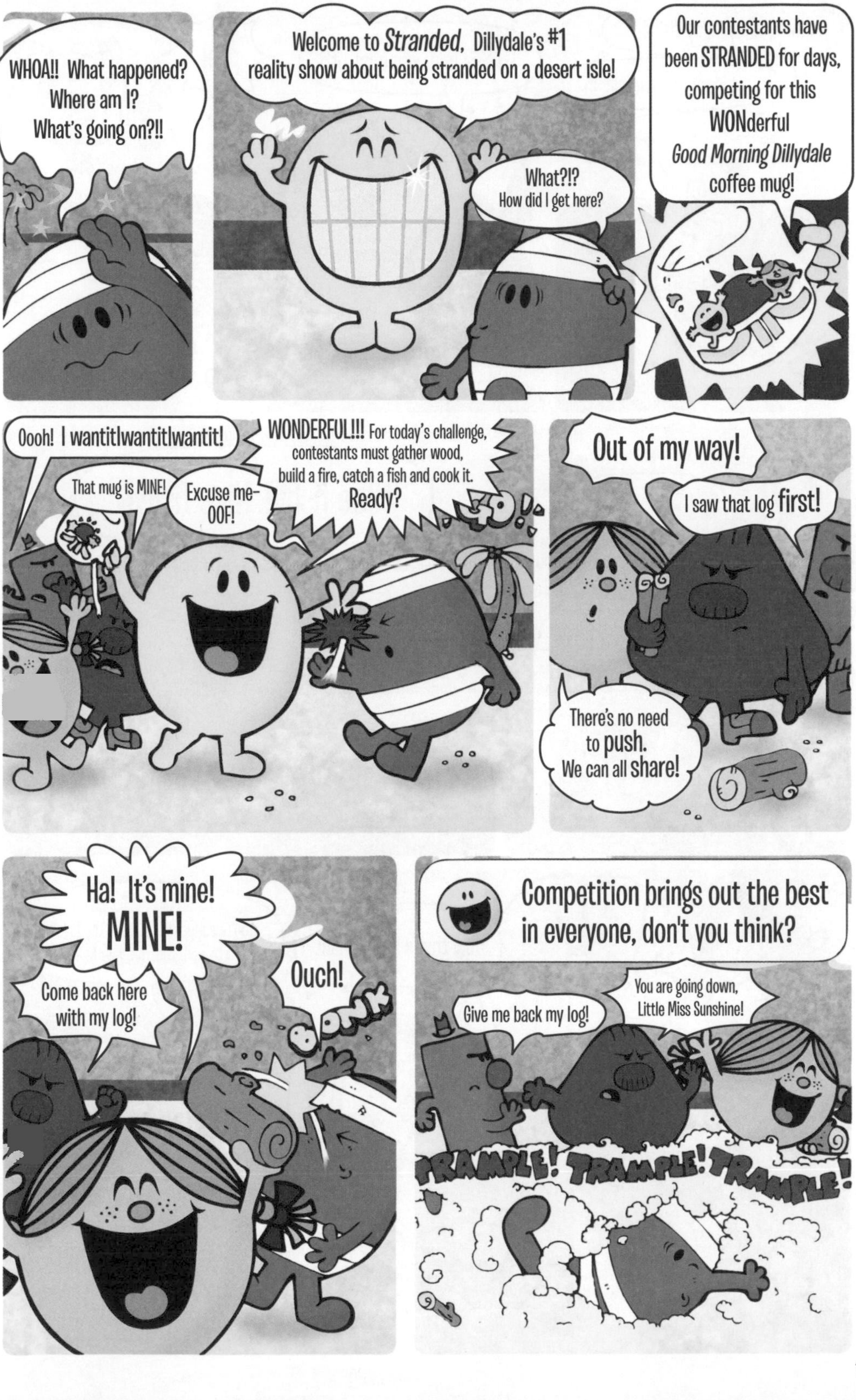
WHOA!! What happened? Where am I? What's going on?!!
Welcome to *Stranded*, Dillydale's #1 reality show about being stranded on a desert isle!
What?!? How did I get here?
Our contestants have been STRANDED for days, competing for this WONderful *Good Morning Dillydale* coffee mug!
Oooh! I wantitIwantitIwantit!
That mug is MINE!
Excuse me— OOF!
WONDERFUL!!! For today's challenge, contestants must gather wood, build a fire, catch a fish and cook it. Ready?
GO!
Out of my way!
I saw that log first!
There's no need to push. We can all share!
Ha! It's mine! MINE!
Come back here with my log!
Ouch!
BONK
Competition brings out the best in everyone, don't you think?
Give me back my log!
You are going down, Little Miss Sunshine!
TRAMPLE! TRAMPLE! TRAMPLE!

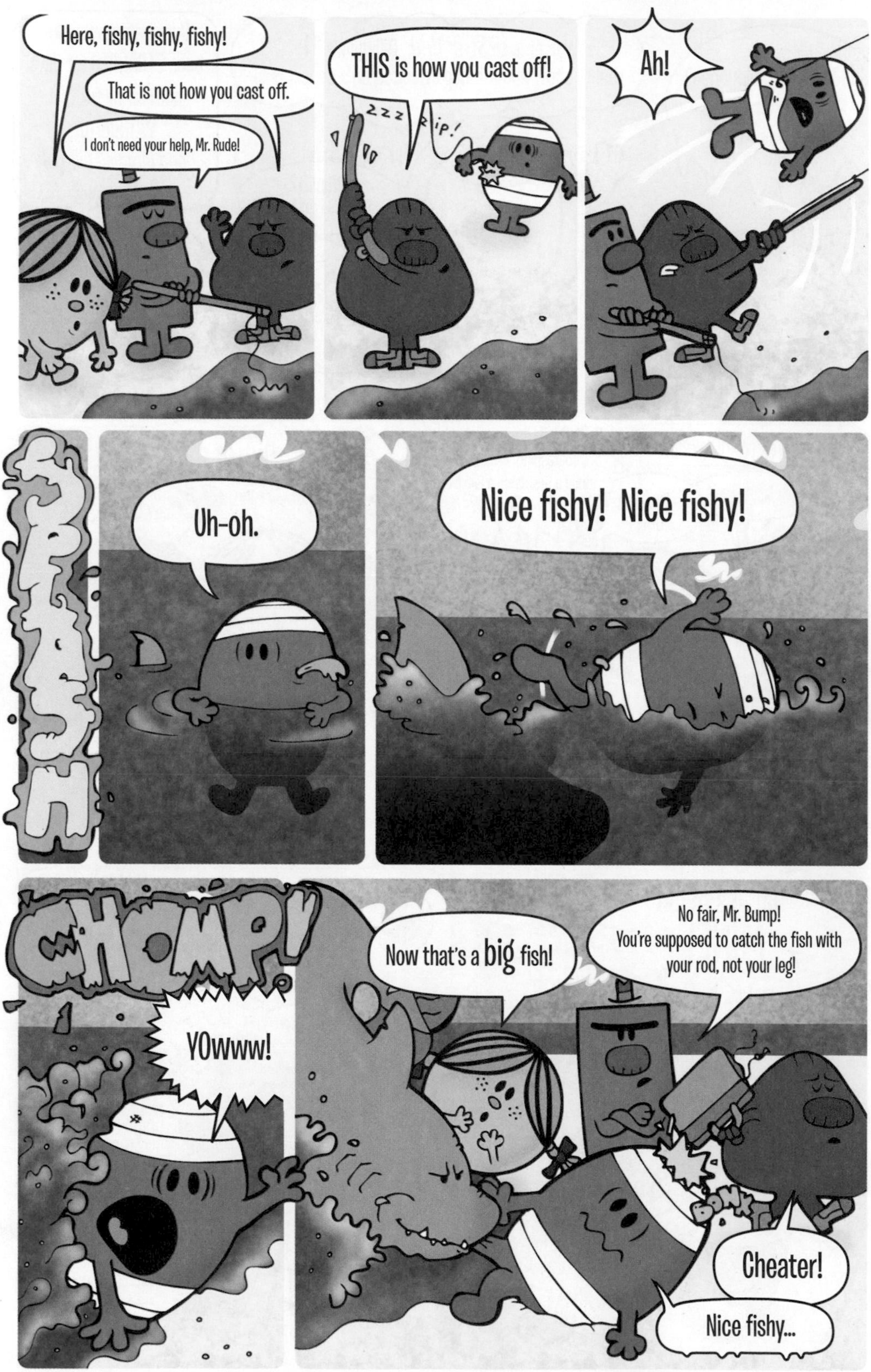
Here, fishy, fishy, fishy!
That is not how you cast off.
I don't need your help, Mr. Rude!
THIS is how you cast off!
Ah!
SPLASH
Uh-oh.
Nice fishy! Nice fishy!
CHOMP!
YOwww!
Now that's a big fish!
No fair, Mr. Bump! You're supposed to catch the fish with your rod, not your leg!
Cheater!
Nice fishy...

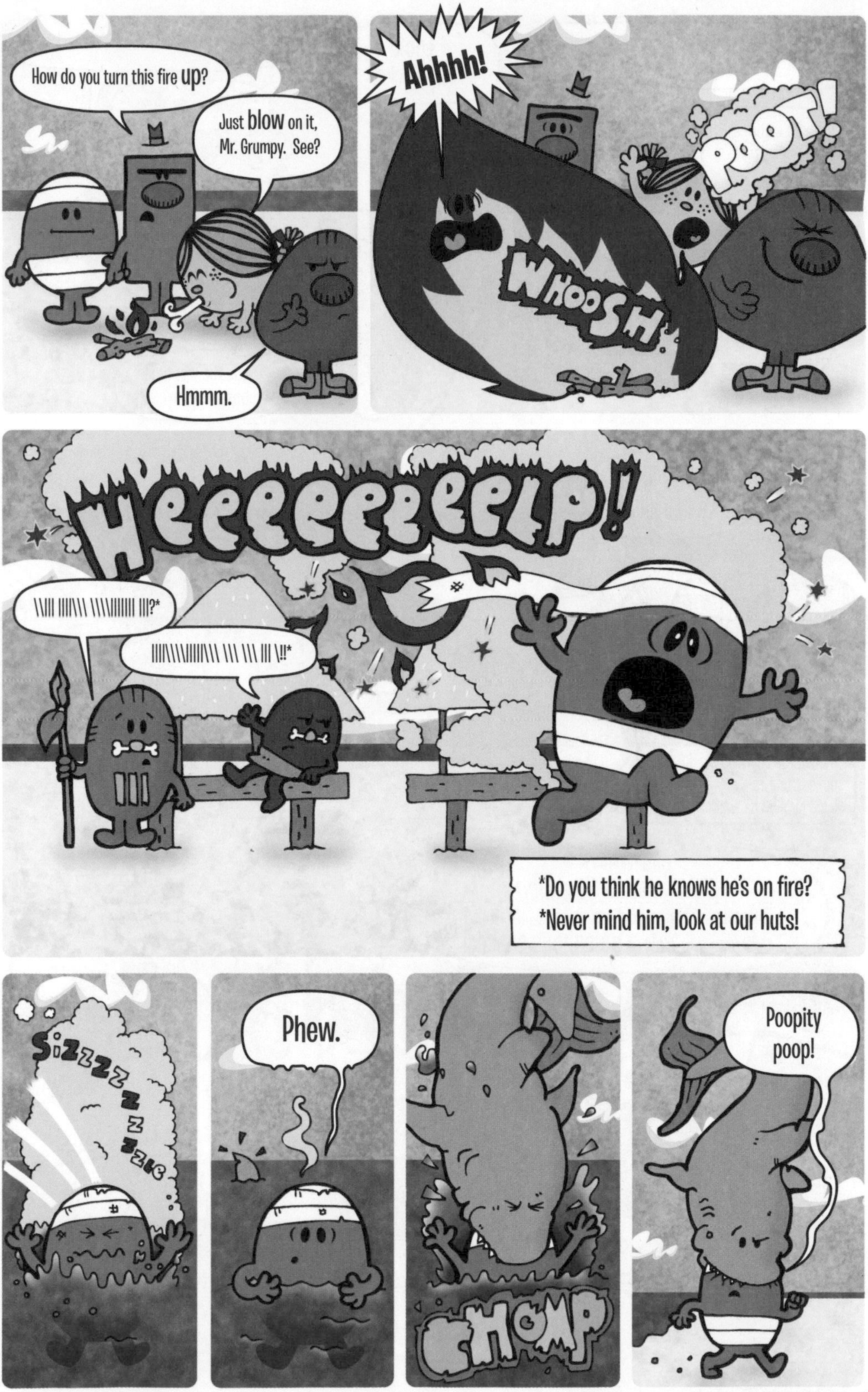

How do you turn this fire up?
Just blow on it, Mr. Grumpy. See?
Hmmm.
Ahhhh!
POOT!
WHOOSH
HEEEEEEEELP!
\\III IIII/\\ \\\\/IIIIIII III?*
IIIII/\\\\IIIIII/\\ \\\ \\\ III \\!!*
*Do you think he knows he's on fire?
*Never mind him, look at our huts!
SIZZZZZZZZLE
Phew.
CHOMP
Poopity poop!

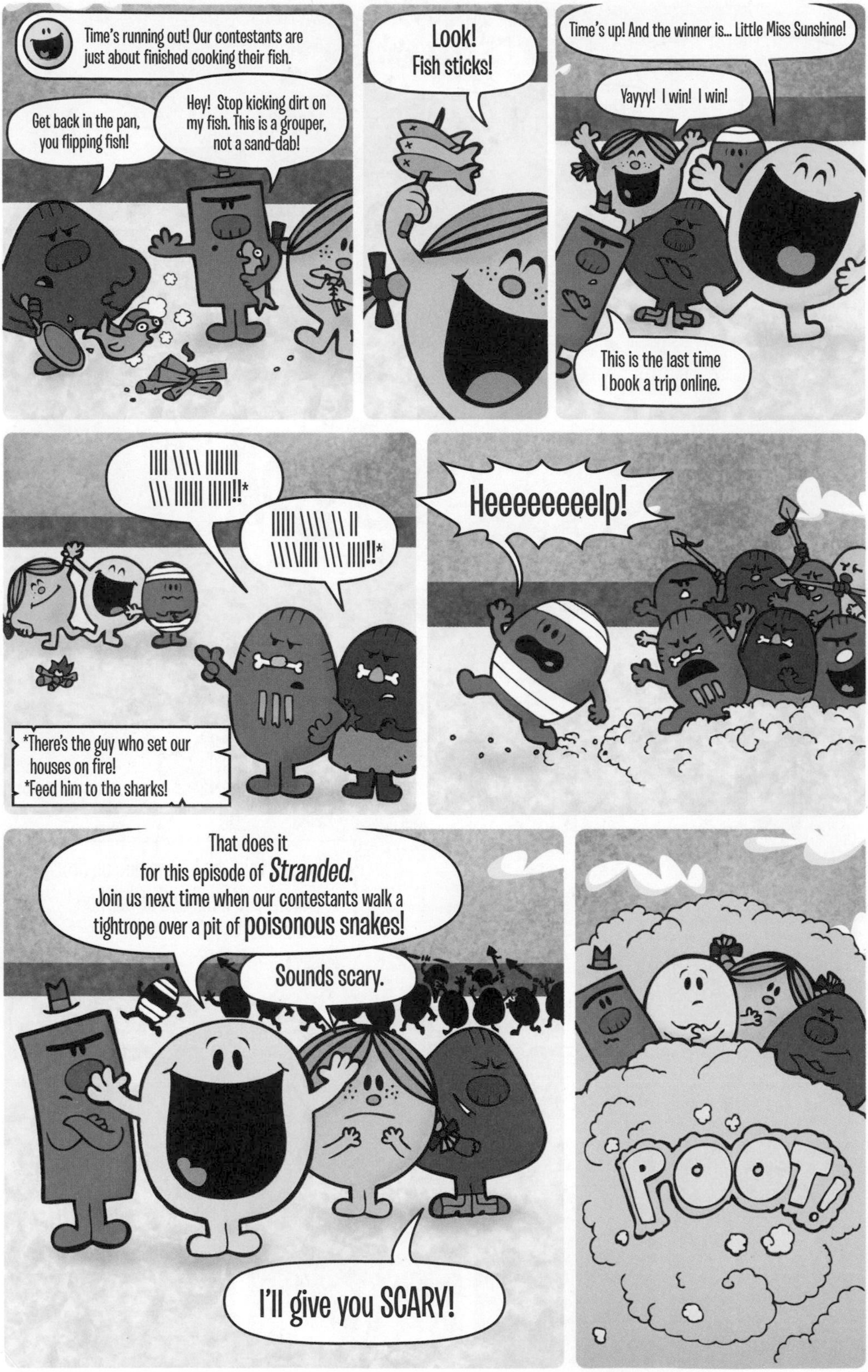
Time's running out! Our contestants are just about finished cooking their fish.
Get back in the pan, you flipping fish!
Hey! Stop kicking dirt on my fish. This is a grouper, not a sand-dab!
Look! Fish sticks!
Time's up! And the winner is... Little Miss Sunshine!
Yayyy! I win! I win!
This is the last time I book a trip online.
|||| \\\\ |||||| \\\ ||||| |||||!!*
||||| \\\\ \\ || \\\\||| \\\ ||||!!*
*There's the guy who set our houses on fire!
*Feed him to the sharks!
Heeeeeeeelp!
That does it for this episode of *Stranded*. Join us next time when our contestants walk a tightrope over a pit of poisonous snakes!
Sounds scary.
I'll give you SCARY!
POOT!

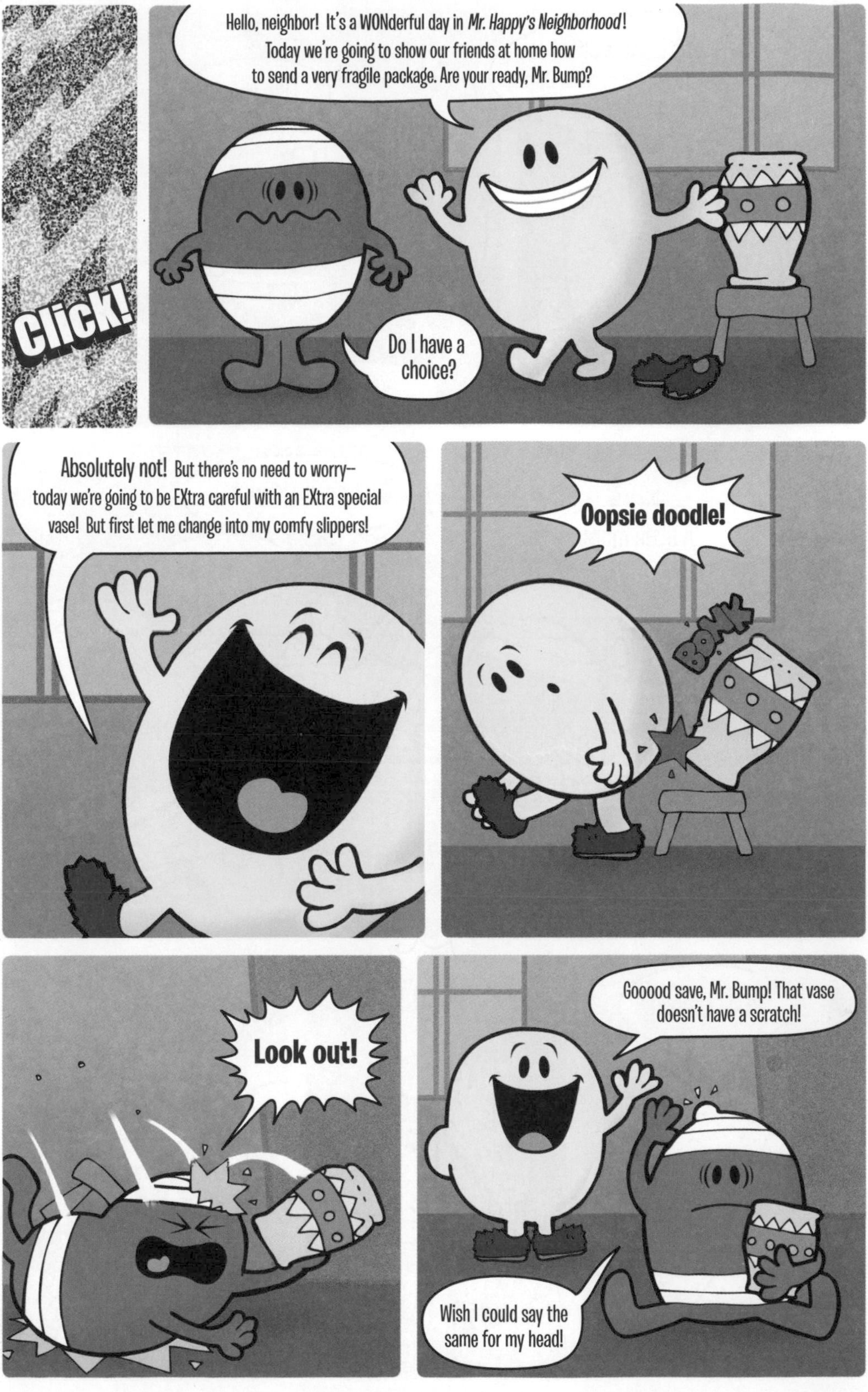
Click!
Hello, neighbor! It's a WONderful day in *Mr. Happy's Neighborhood*! Today we're going to show our friends at home how to send a very fragile package. Are your ready, Mr. Bump?
Do I have a choice?
Absolutely not! But there's no need to worry– today we're going to be EXtra careful with an EXtra special vase! But first let me change into my comfy slippers!
Oopsie doodle!
BONK
Look out!
Gooood save, Mr. Bump! That vase doesn't have a scratch!
Wish I could say the same for my head!

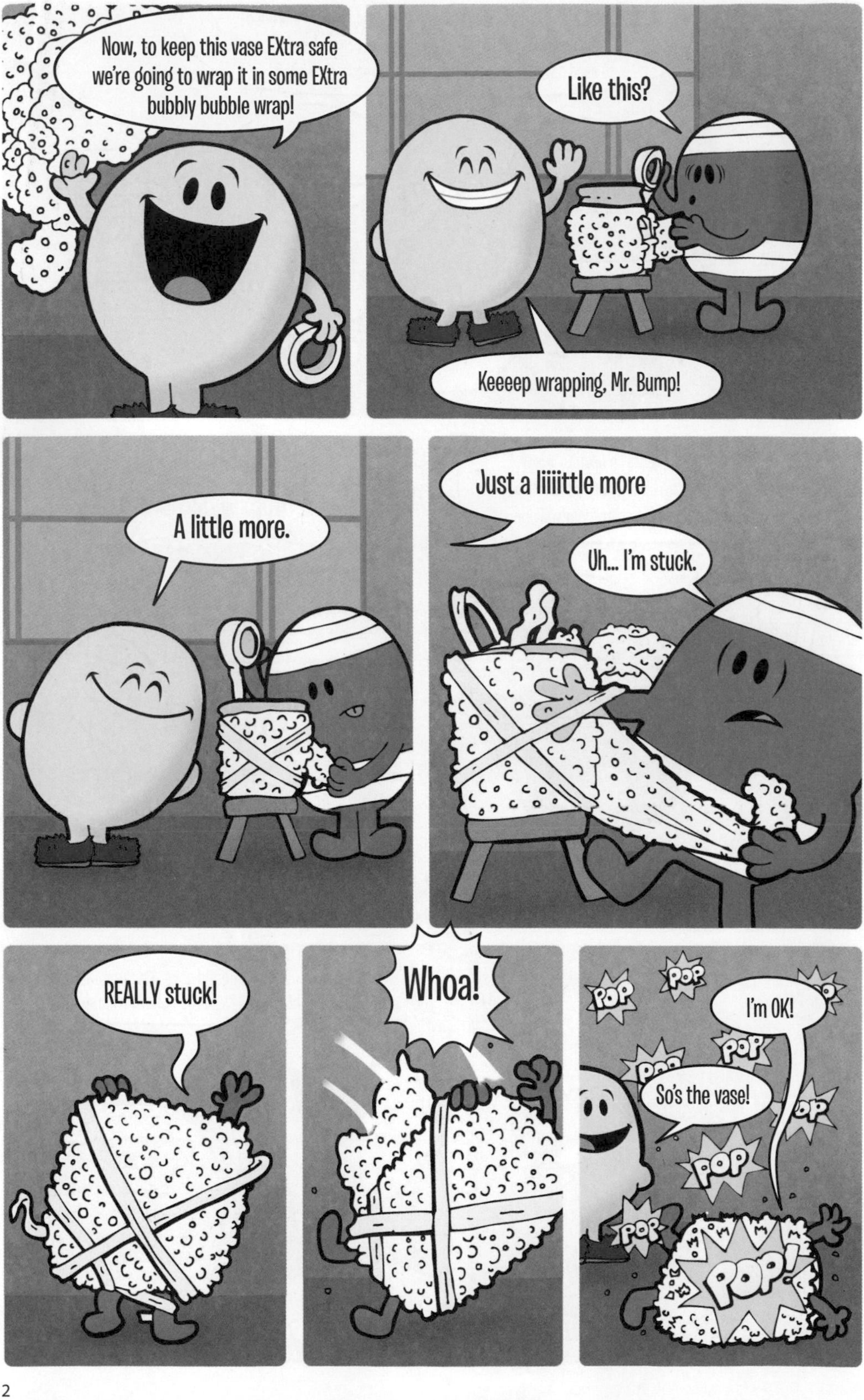

Now, to keep this vase EXtra safe we're going to wrap it in some EXtra bubbly bubble wrap!
Like this?
Keeeep wrapping, Mr. Bump!
A little more.
Just a liiiittle more
Uh... I'm stuck.
REALLY stuck!
Whoa!
POP
POP
I'm OK!
POP
So's the vase!
POP
POP
POP!

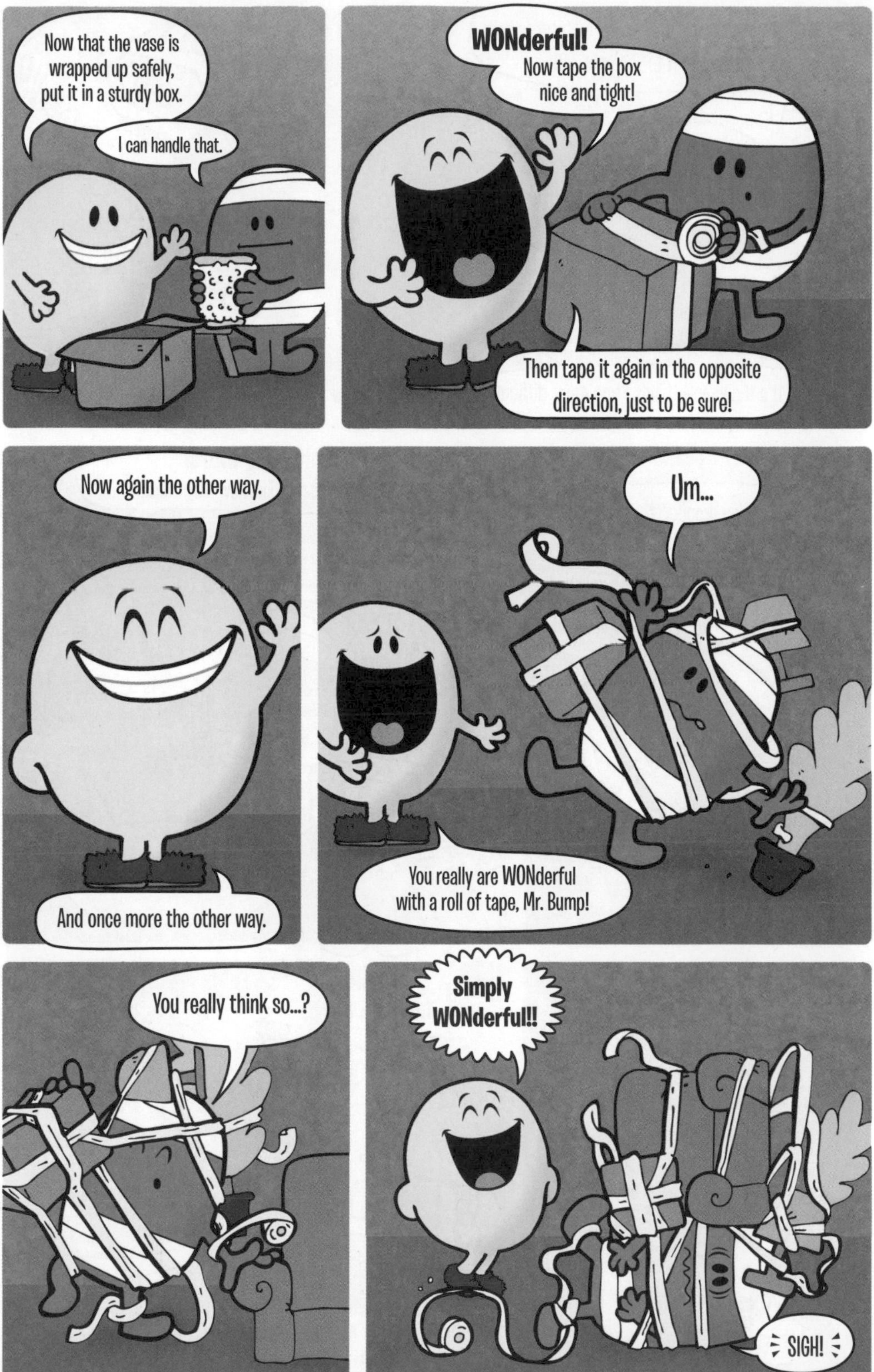

Now that the vase is wrapped up safely, put it in a sturdy box.
I can handle that.
WONderful!
Now tape the box nice and tight!
Then tape it again in the opposite direction, just to be sure!
Now again the other way.
And once more the other way.
Um...
You really are WONderful with a roll of tape, Mr. Bump!
You really think so...?
Simply WONderful!!
SIGH!

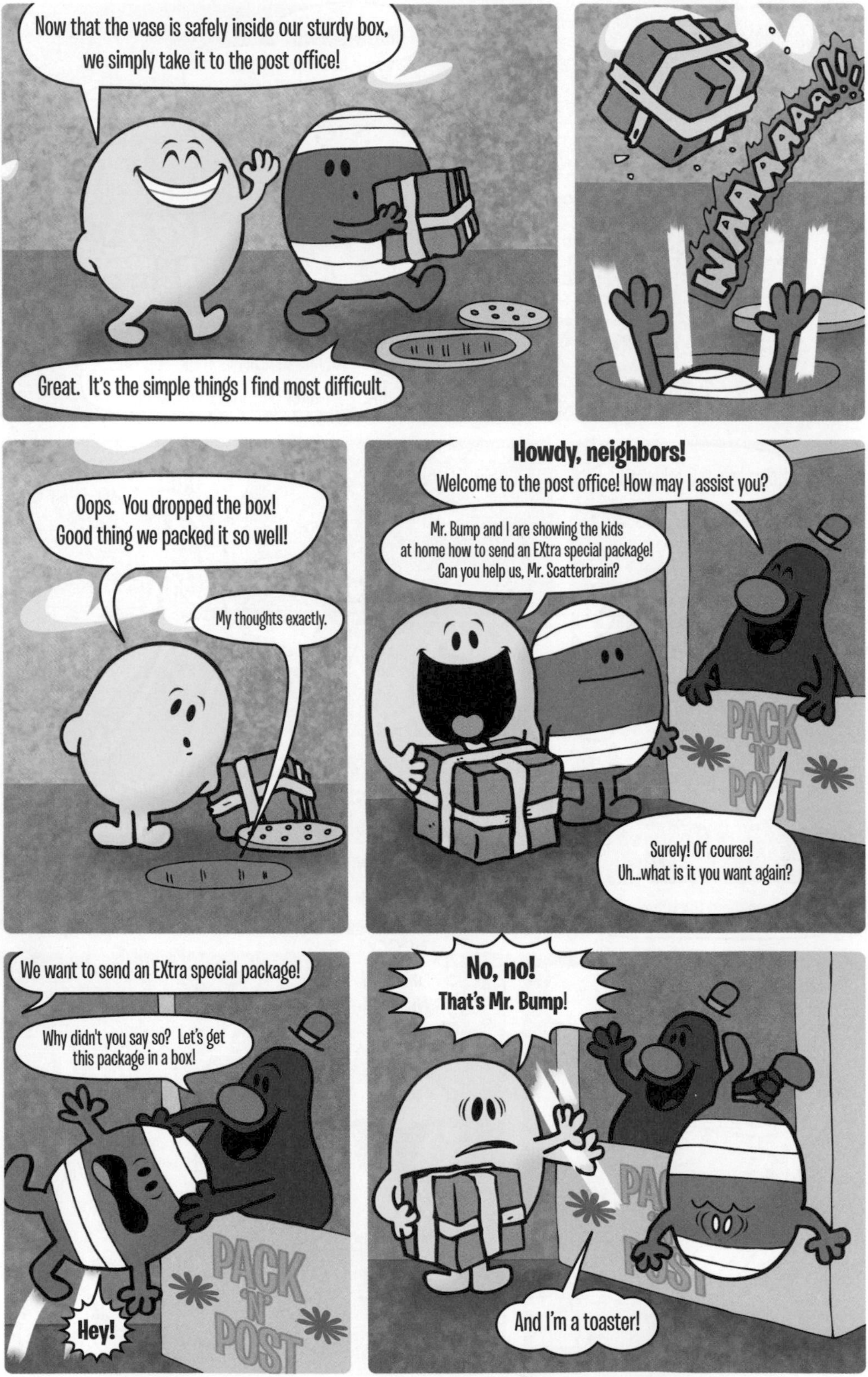

Now that the vase is safely inside our sturdy box, we simply take it to the post office!
Great. It's the simple things I find most difficult.
WAAAAAA!!!
Oops. You dropped the box! Good thing we packed it so well!
My thoughts exactly.
Howdy, neighbors!
Welcome to the post office! How may I assist you?
Mr. Bump and I are showing the kids at home how to send an EXtra special package! Can you help us, Mr. Scatterbrain?
PACK 'N' POST
Surely! Of course! Uh...what is it you want again?
We want to send an EXtra special package!
Why didn't you say so? Let's get this package in a box!
PACK 'N' POST
Hey!
No, no!
That's Mr. Bump!
And I'm a toaster!

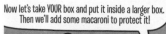
Now let's take YOUR box and put it inside a larger box.
Then we'll add some macaroni to protect it!

WONderful! And that machine does all the work?

Either that or it makes pickles...

Look at all those doodads and thingamajigs! It must take years to learn how to operate all this!

I just started this morning! Now which one's the hamster?

Let's try this one.

Now we're cookin'!

Wah!!

SPROING!!

Now we'll just mark it "Fragile..."

Yow!

FRAGILE

...and load it up to be shipped!

Now where did Mr. Bump go? He's missing everything!

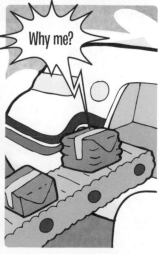

Why me?

15

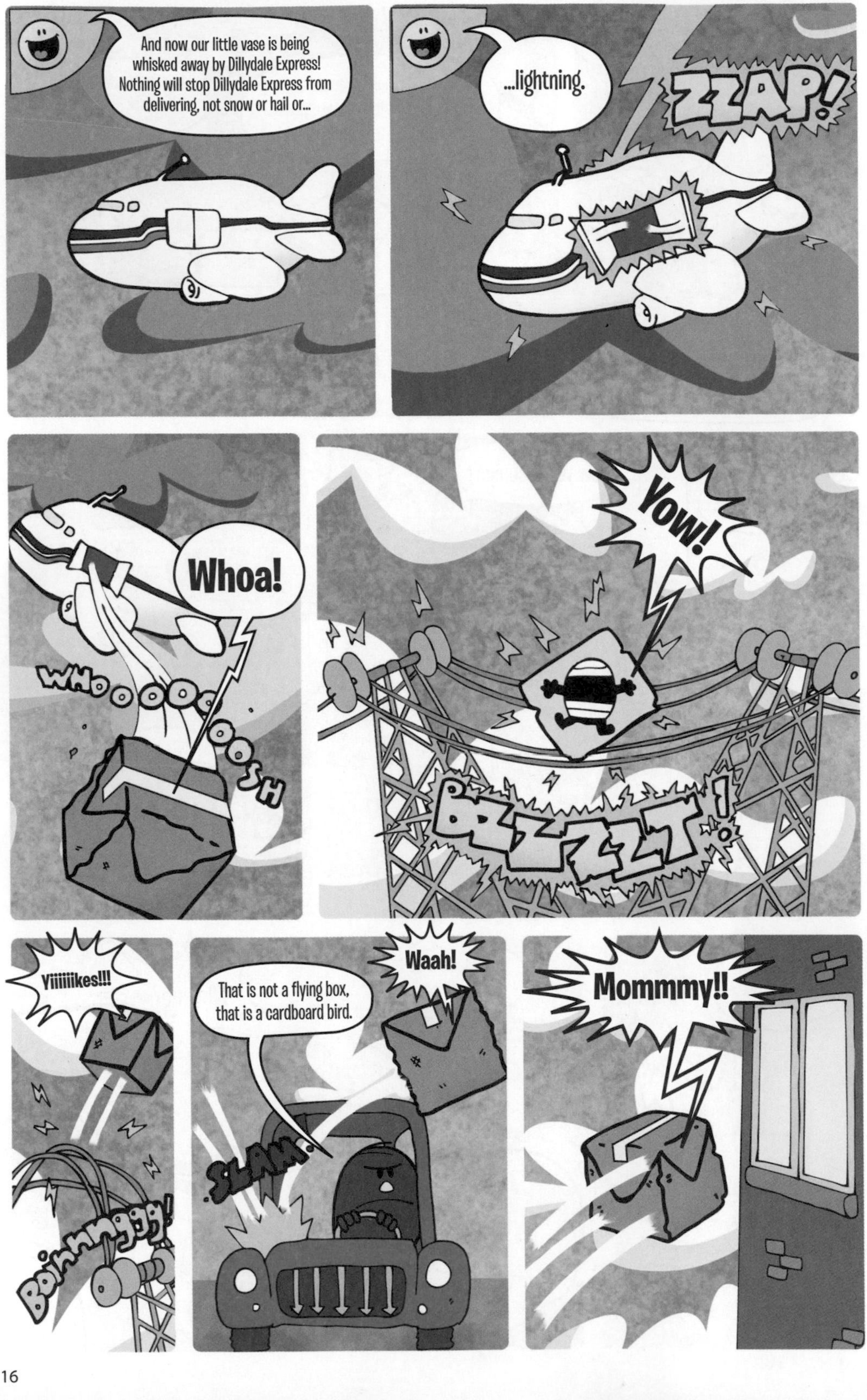
And now our little vase is being whisked away by Dillydale Express! Nothing will stop Dillydale Express from delivering, not snow or hail or...
...lightning.
ZZAP!
Whoa!
WHOOOOOOOSH
Yow!
BZZZT!
Yiiiiiikes!!!
Boiinnnggg!
That is not a flying box, that is a cardboard bird.
SLAM
Waah!
Mommmy!!

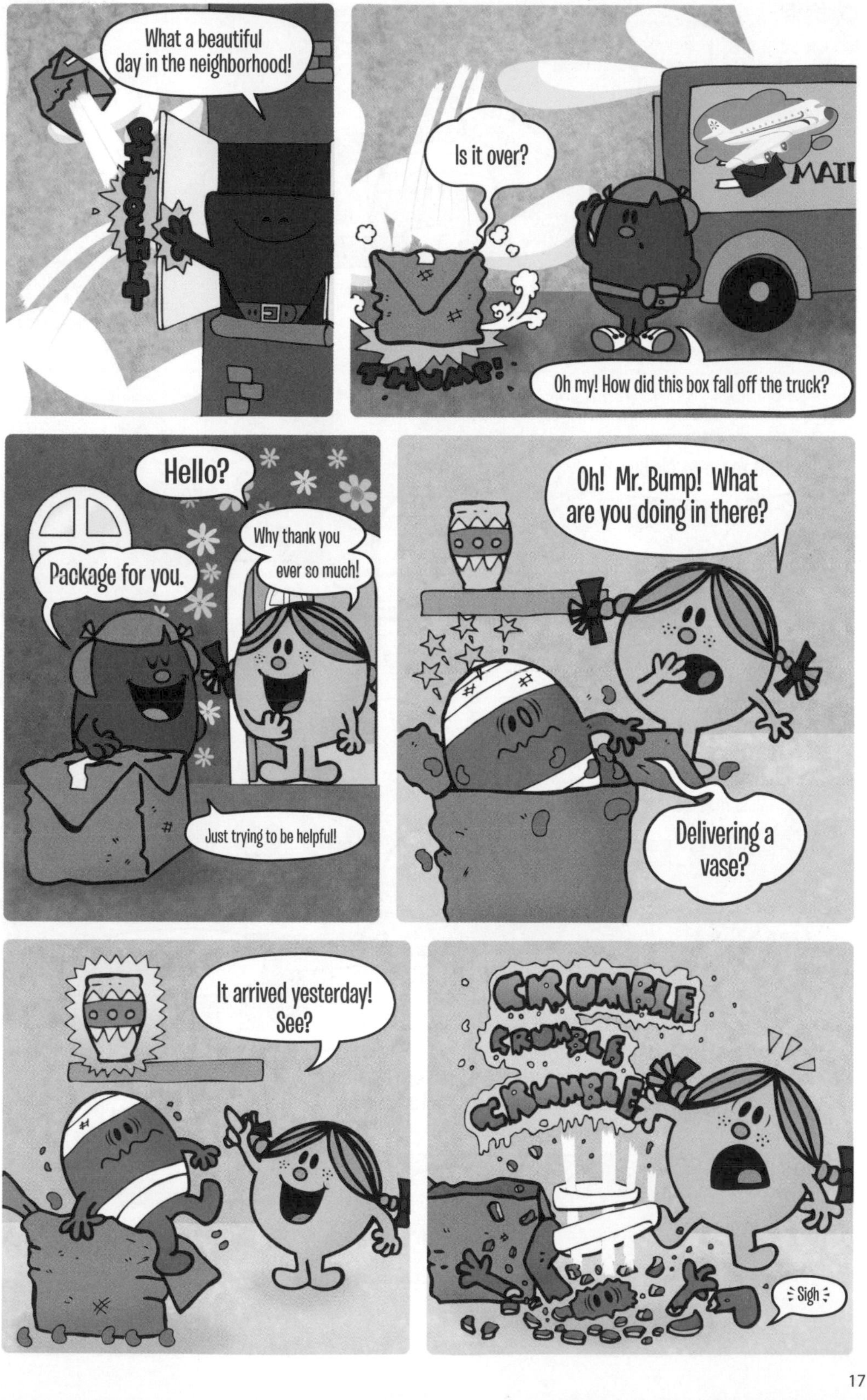
What a beautiful day in the neighborhood!
RICOCHET
Is it over?
MAIL
THUMP!
Oh my! How did this box fall off the truck?
Hello?
Package for you.
Why thank you ever so much!
Just trying to be helpful!
Oh! Mr. Bump! What are you doing in there?
Delivering a vase?
It arrived yesterday! See?
CRUMBLE
CRUMBLE
CRUMBLE
Sigh

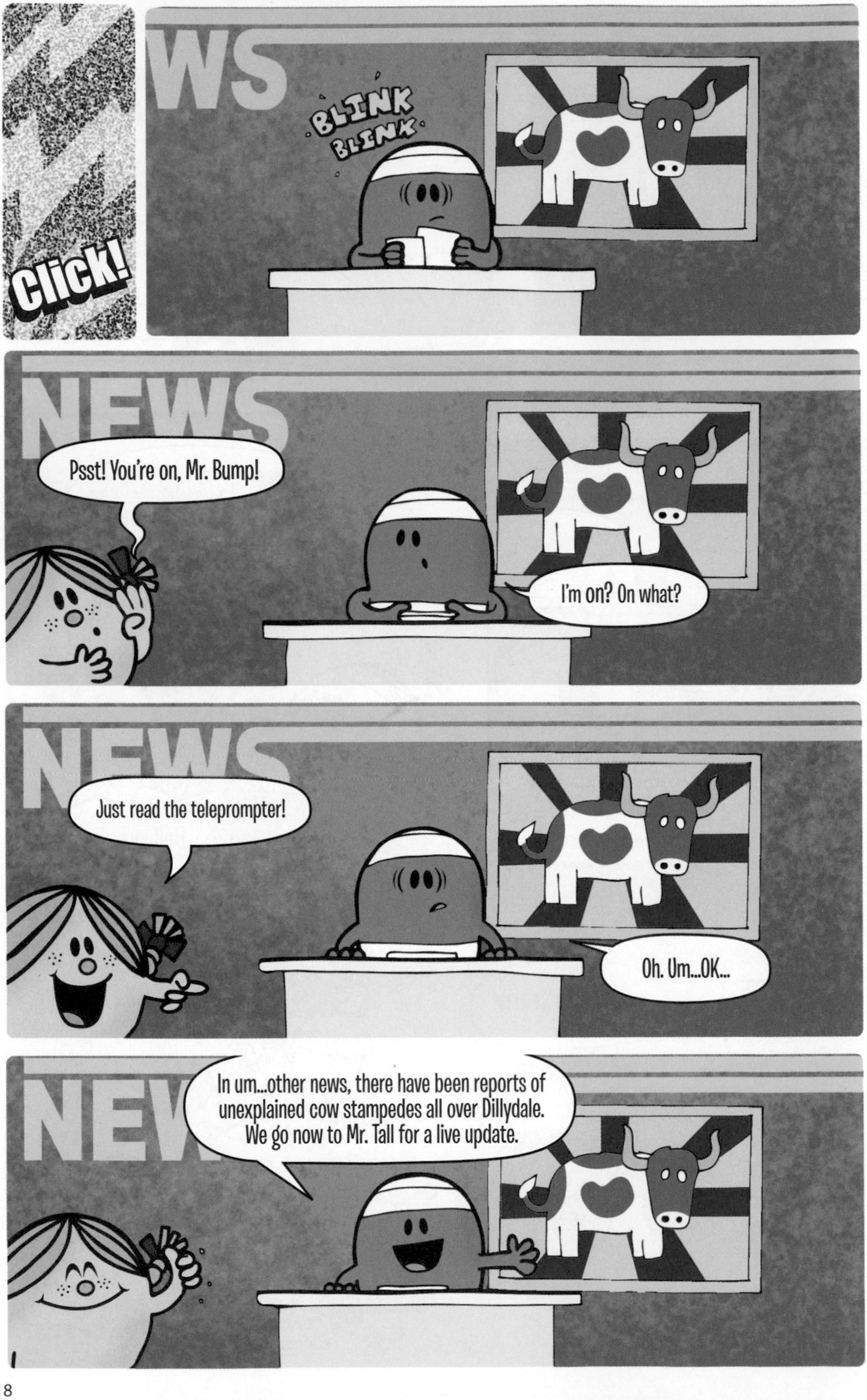
Click!
NEWS
BLINK
BLINK
NEWS
Psst! You're on, Mr. Bump!
I'm on? On what?
NEWS
Just read the teleprompter!
Oh. Um...OK...
NEWS
In um...other news, there have been reports of unexplained cow stampedes all over Dillydale. We go now to Mr. Tall for a live update.

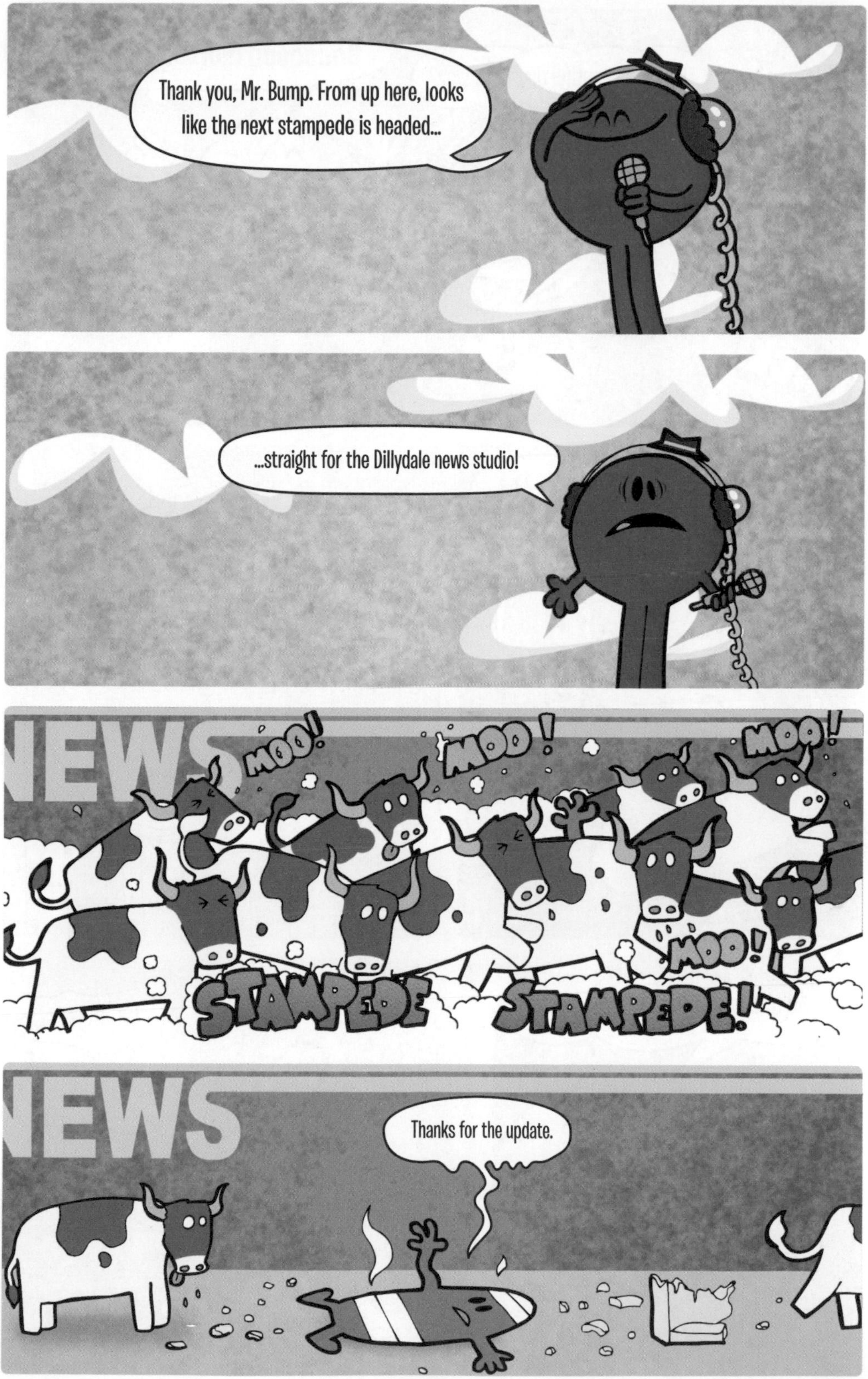
Thank you, Mr. Bump. From up here, looks like the next stampede is headed...
...straight for the Dillydale news studio!
NEWS
MOO!
MOO!
MOO!
MOO!
STAMPEDE
STAMPEDE!
NEWS
Thanks for the update.

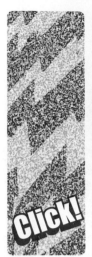

Click!

Isn't it a beautiful day, Mr. Happy?

Goooood morning, Dillydale!

It most certainly is. A WONderful day. **Wooooonderful!**

We've got all kinds of SUPER things planned for today! Later, Mr. Bounce will take us on a tour of Dillydale's newest roller coaster!

Wheeeee!

WONderful! And then Little Miss Whoops is going to show us how to clean a chandelier!

Whoops.

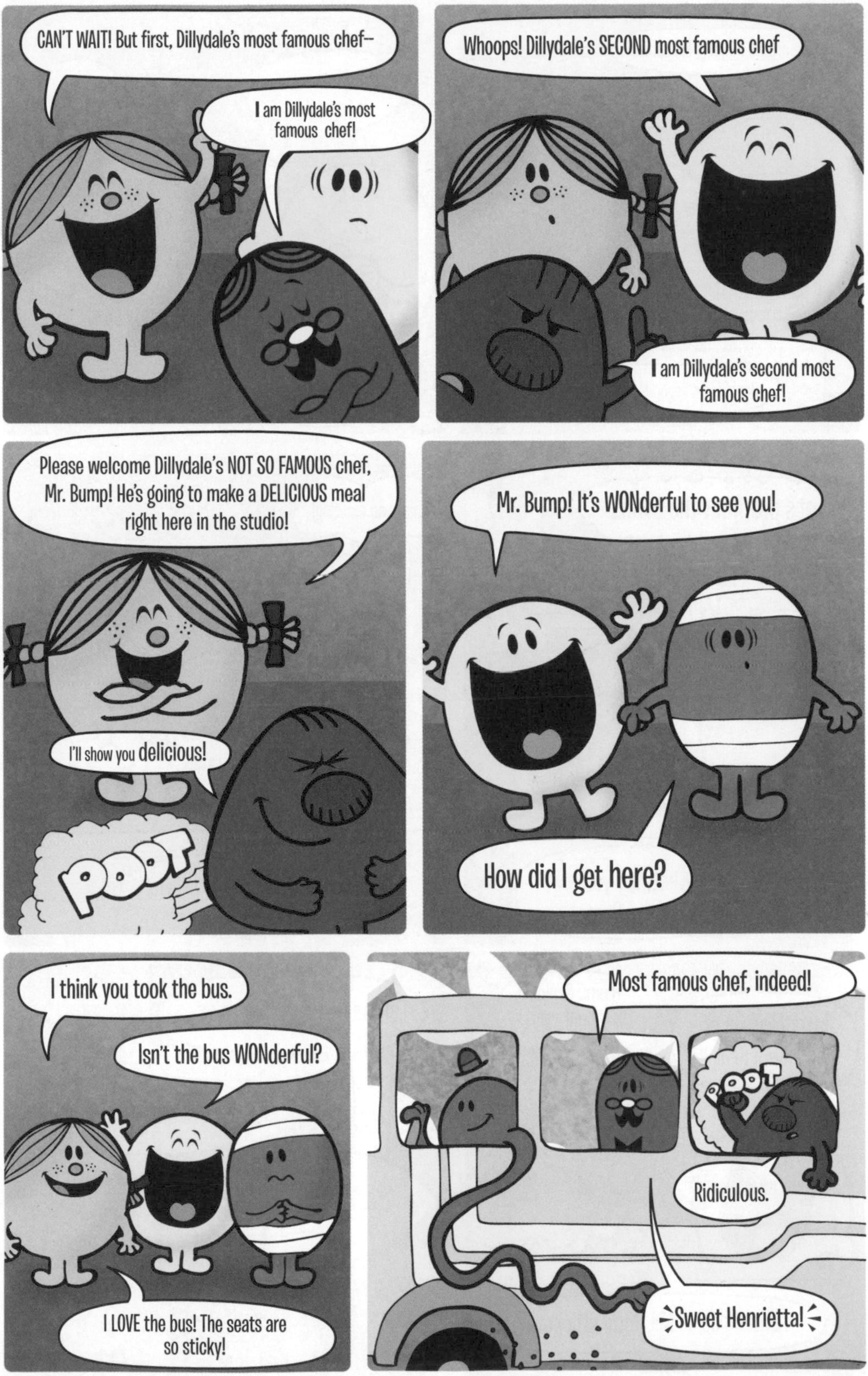
CAN'T WAIT! But first, Dillydale's most famous chef--
I am Dillydale's most famous chef!
Whoops! Dillydale's SECOND most famous chef
I am Dillydale's second most famous chef!
Please welcome Dillydale's NOT SO FAMOUS chef, Mr. Bump! He's going to make a DELICIOUS meal right here in the studio!
I'll show you delicious!
POOT
Mr. Bump! It's WONderful to see you!
How did I get here?
I think you took the bus.
Isn't the bus WONderful?
I LOVE the bus! The seats are so sticky!
Most famous chef, indeed!
POOT
Ridiculous.
Sweet Henrietta!

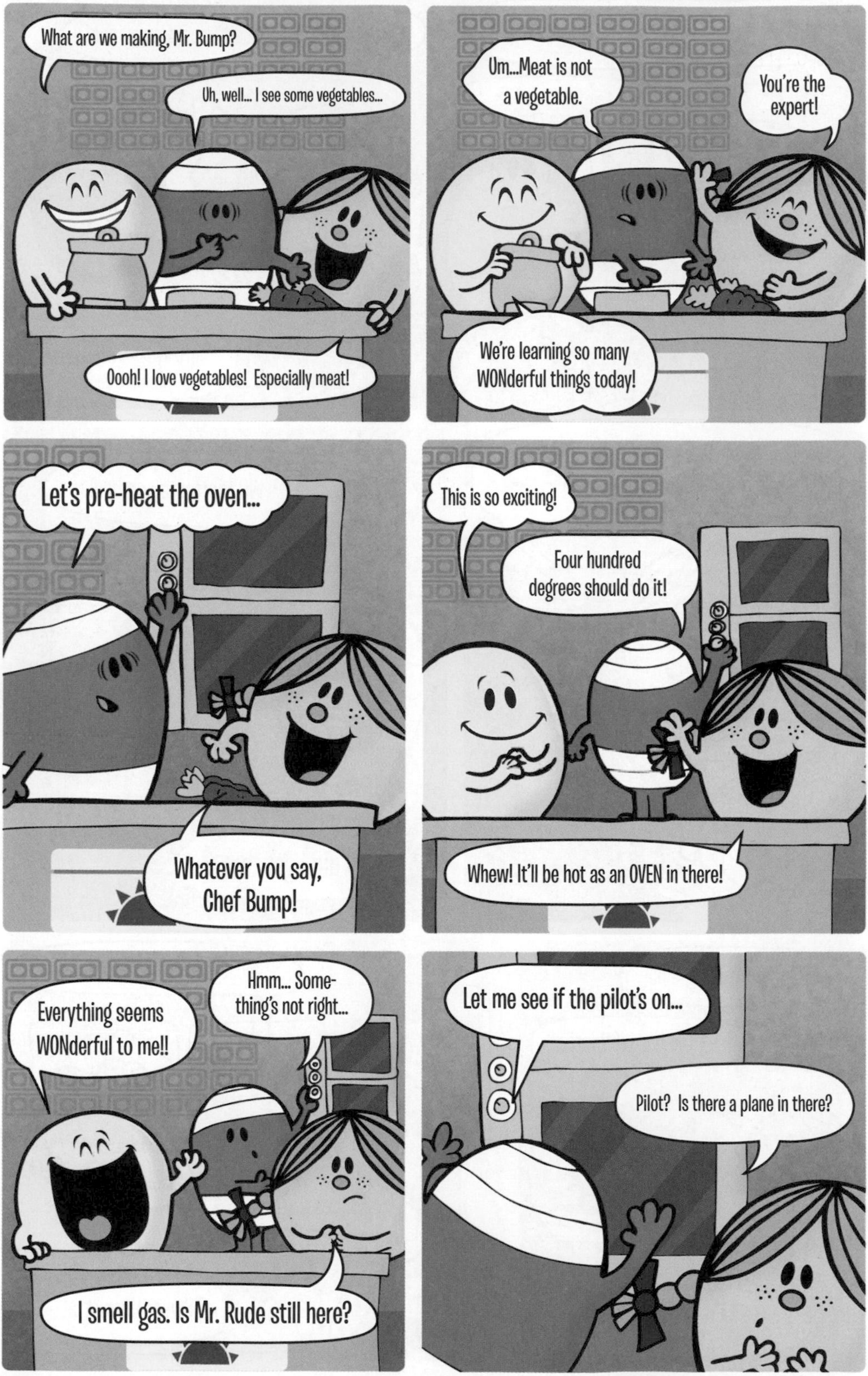
What are we making, Mr. Bump?
Uh, well... I see some vegetables...
Oooh! I love vegetables! Especially meat!
Um...Meat is not a vegetable.
You're the expert!
We're learning so many WONderful things today!
Let's pre-heat the oven...
Whatever you say, Chef Bump!
This is so exciting!
Four hundred degrees should do it!
Whew! It'll be hot as an OVEN in there!
Everything seems WONderful to me!!
Hmm... Something's not right...
I smell gas. Is Mr. Rude still here?
Let me see if the pilot's on...
Pilot? Is there a plane in there?

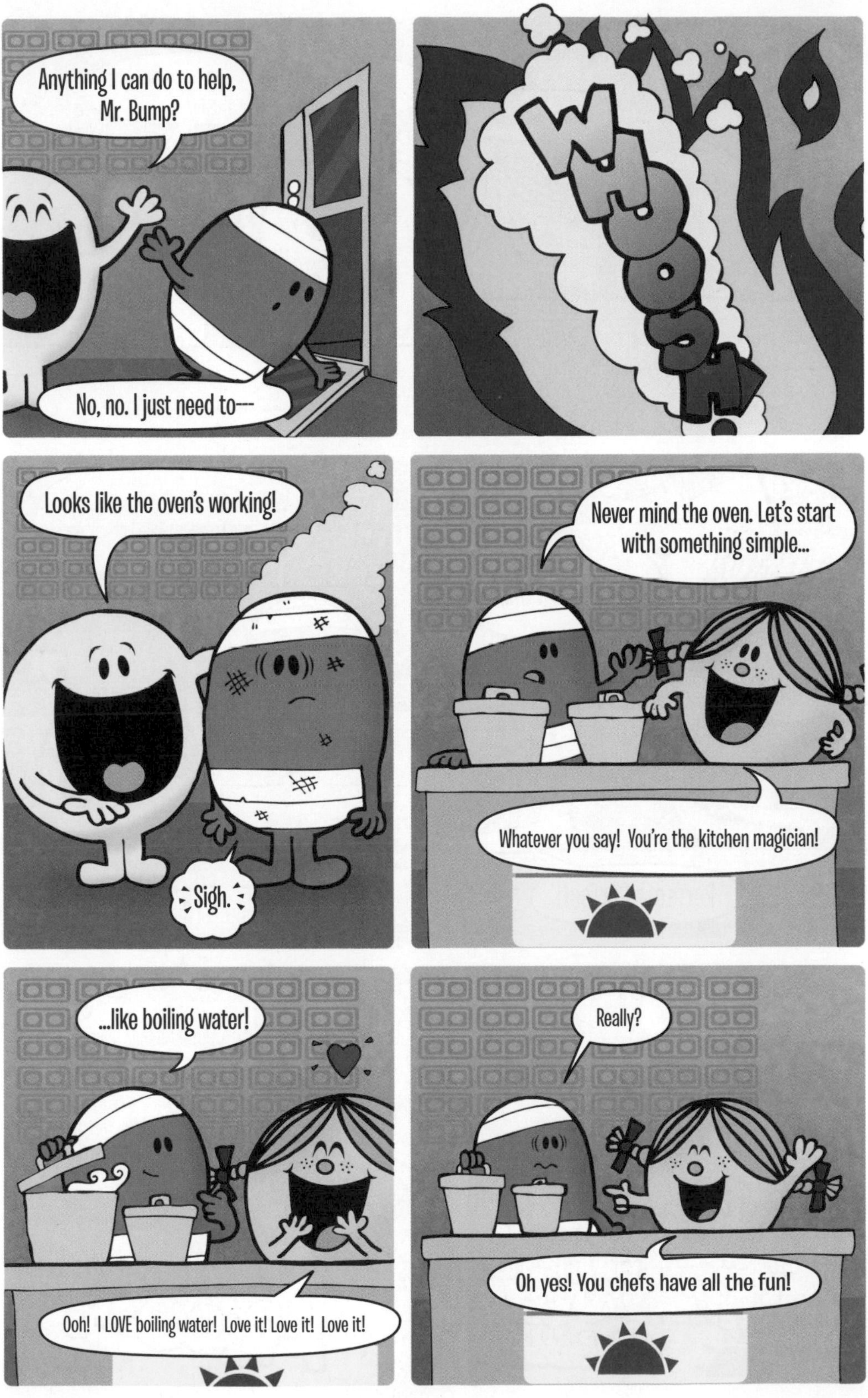
Anything I can do to help, Mr. Bump?
No, no. I just need to---
WHOOSH!
Looks like the oven's working!
Sigh.
Never mind the oven. Let's start with something simple...
Whatever you say! You're the kitchen magician!
...like boiling water!
Ooh! I LOVE boiling water! Love it! Love it! Love it!
Really?
Oh yes! You chefs have all the fun!

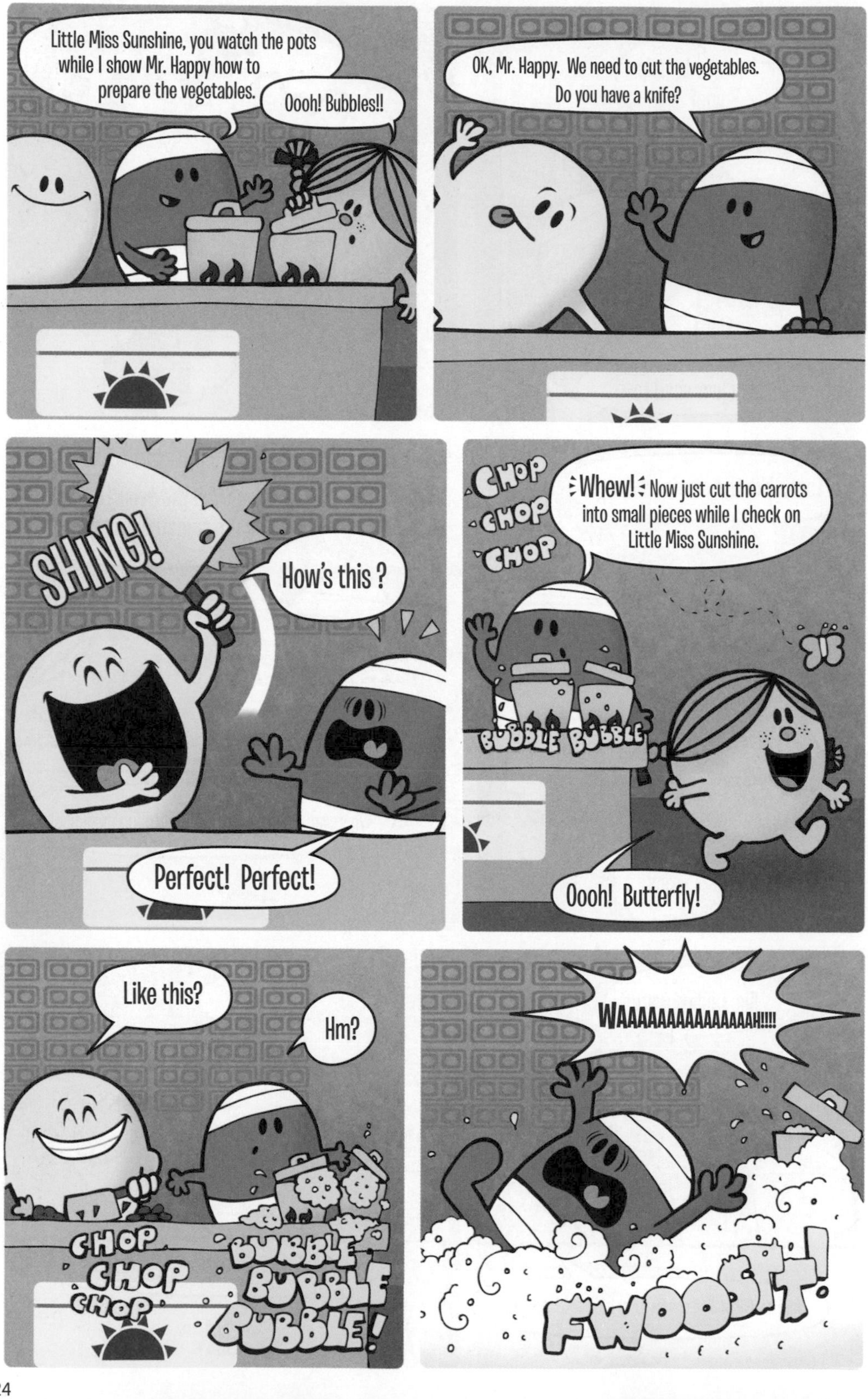
Little Miss Sunshine, you watch the pots while I show Mr. Happy how to prepare the vegetables.
Oooh! Bubbles!!
OK, Mr. Happy. We need to cut the vegetables. Do you have a knife?
SHING!
How's this ?
Perfect! Perfect!
CHOP
CHOP
CHOP
Whew! Now just cut the carrots into small pieces while I check on Little Miss Sunshine.
BUBBLE BUBBLE
Oooh! Butterfly!
Like this?
Hm?
CHOP
CHOP
CHOP
BUBBLE
BUBBLE
BUBBLE!
WAAAAAAAAAAAAAAAH!!!!
FWOOSTT!

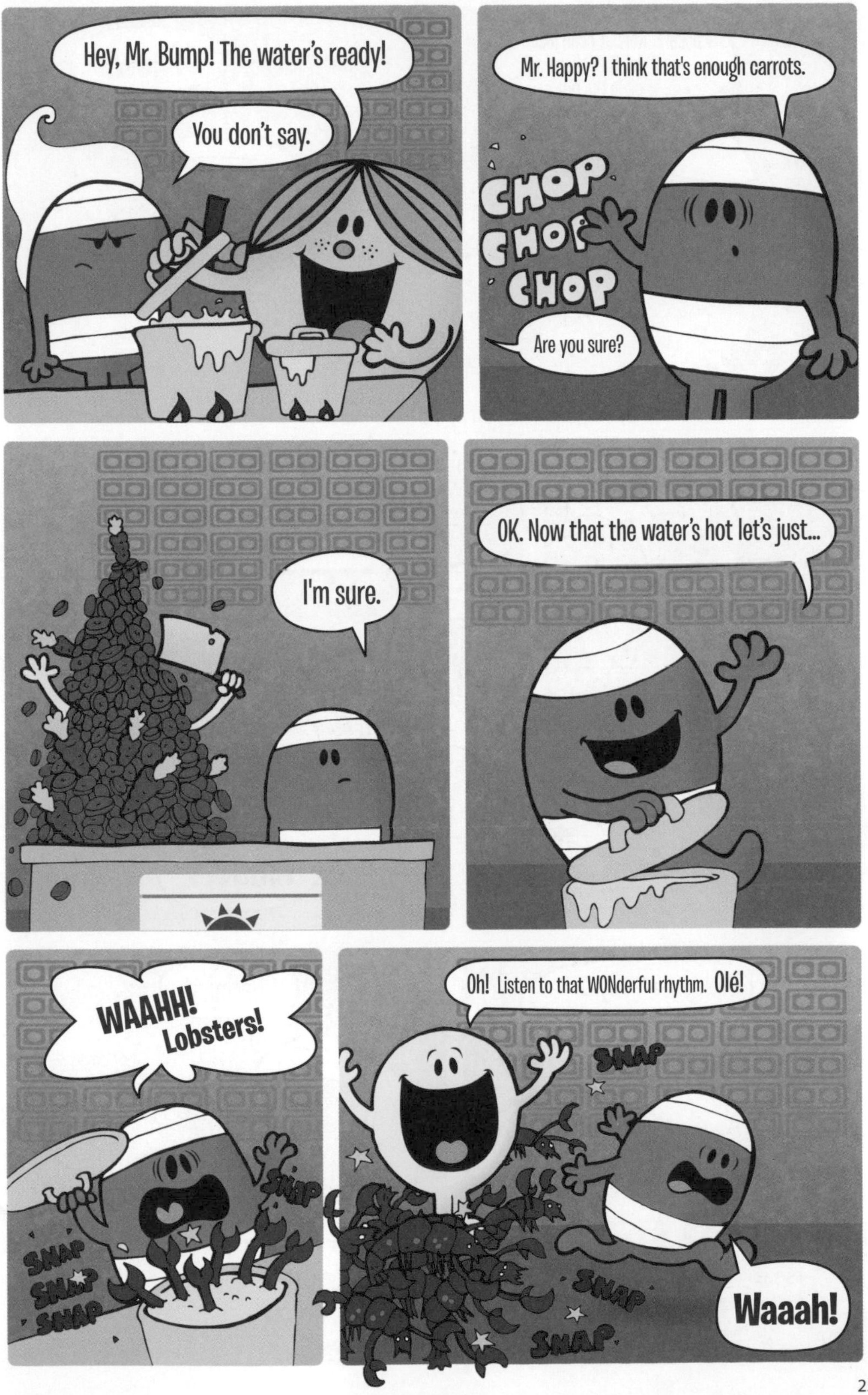
Hey, Mr. Bump! The water's ready!
You don't say.
Mr. Happy? I think that's enough carrots.
CHOP CHOP CHOP
Are you sure?
I'm sure.
OK. Now that the water's hot let's just...
WAAHH! Lobsters!
SNAP
SNAP SNAP SNAP
Oh! Listen to that WONderful rhythm. Olé!
SNAP
SNAP
SNAP
Waaah!

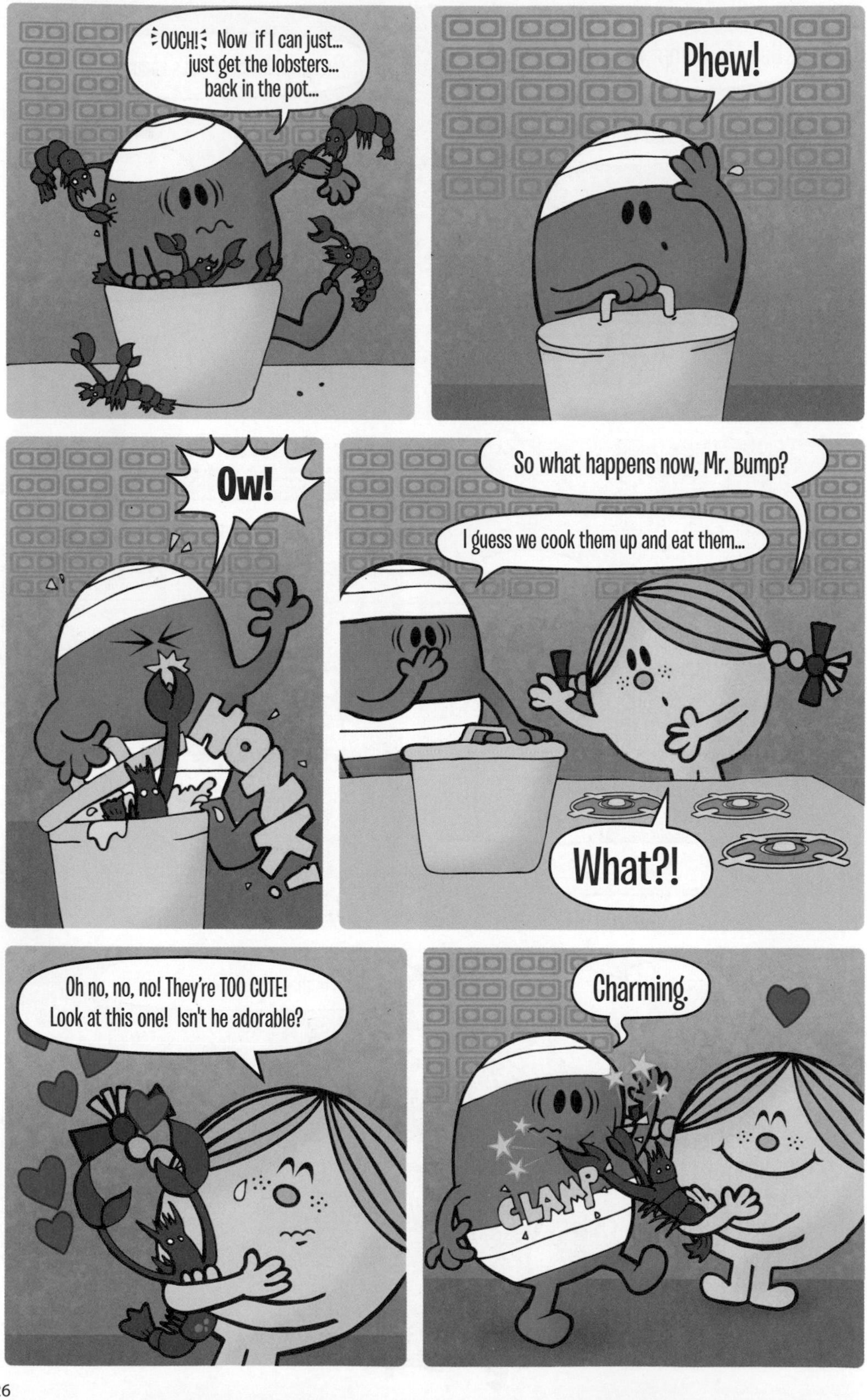
OUCH! Now if I can just... just get the lobsters... back in the pot...
Phew!
Ow!
HONK!
So what happens now, Mr. Bump?
I guess we cook them up and eat them...
What?!
Oh no, no, no! They're TOO CUTE! Look at this one! Isn't he adorable?
Charming.
CLAMP

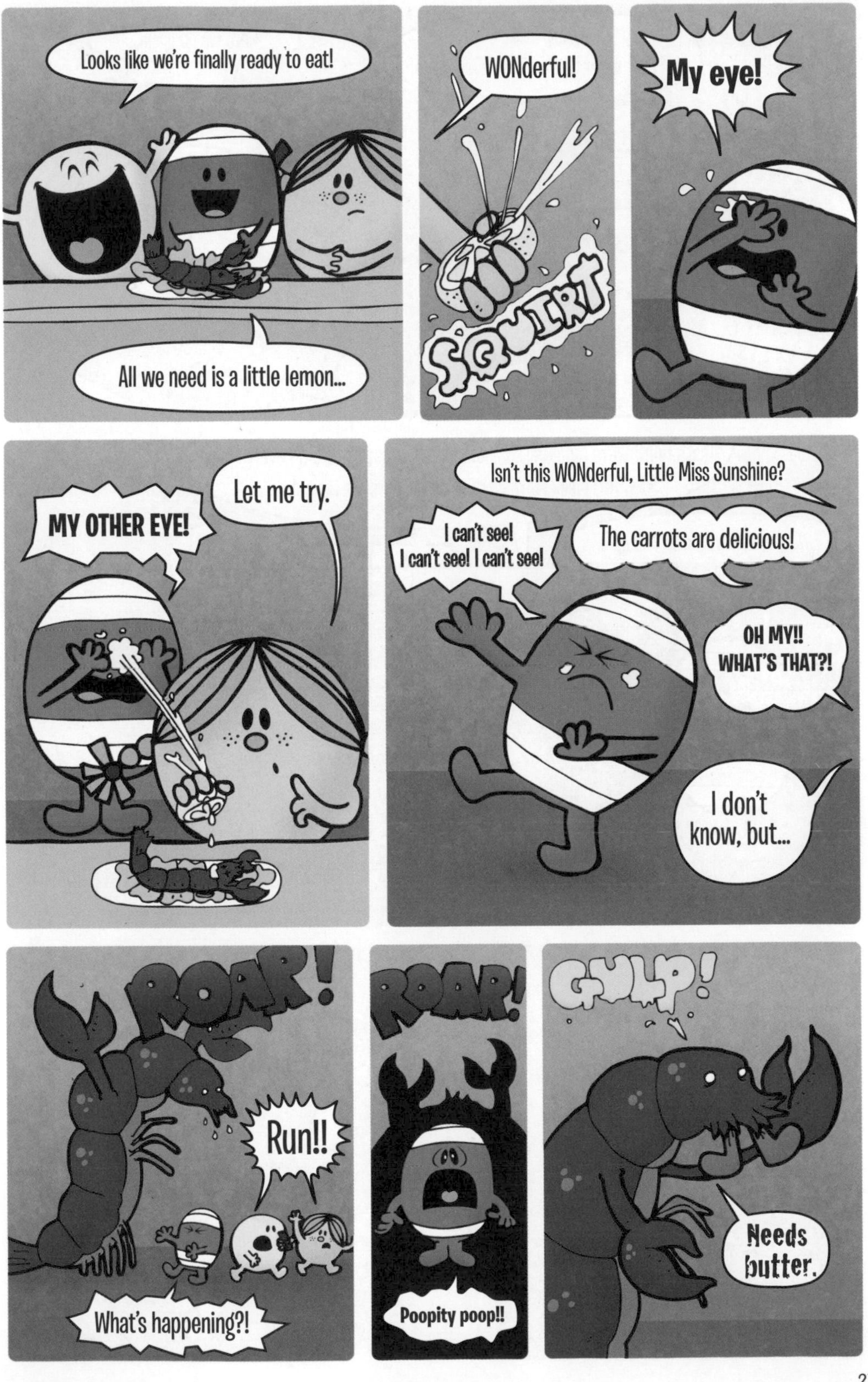

Looks like we're finally ready to eat!
All we need is a little lemon...
WONderful!
SQUIRT
My eye!
MY OTHER EYE!
Let me try.
Isn't this WONderful, Little Miss Sunshine?
I can't see! I can't see! I can't see!
The carrots are delicious!
OH MY!! WHAT'S THAT?!
I don't know, but...
ROAR!
Run!!
What's happening?!
ROAR!
Poopity poop!!
GULP!
Needs butter.

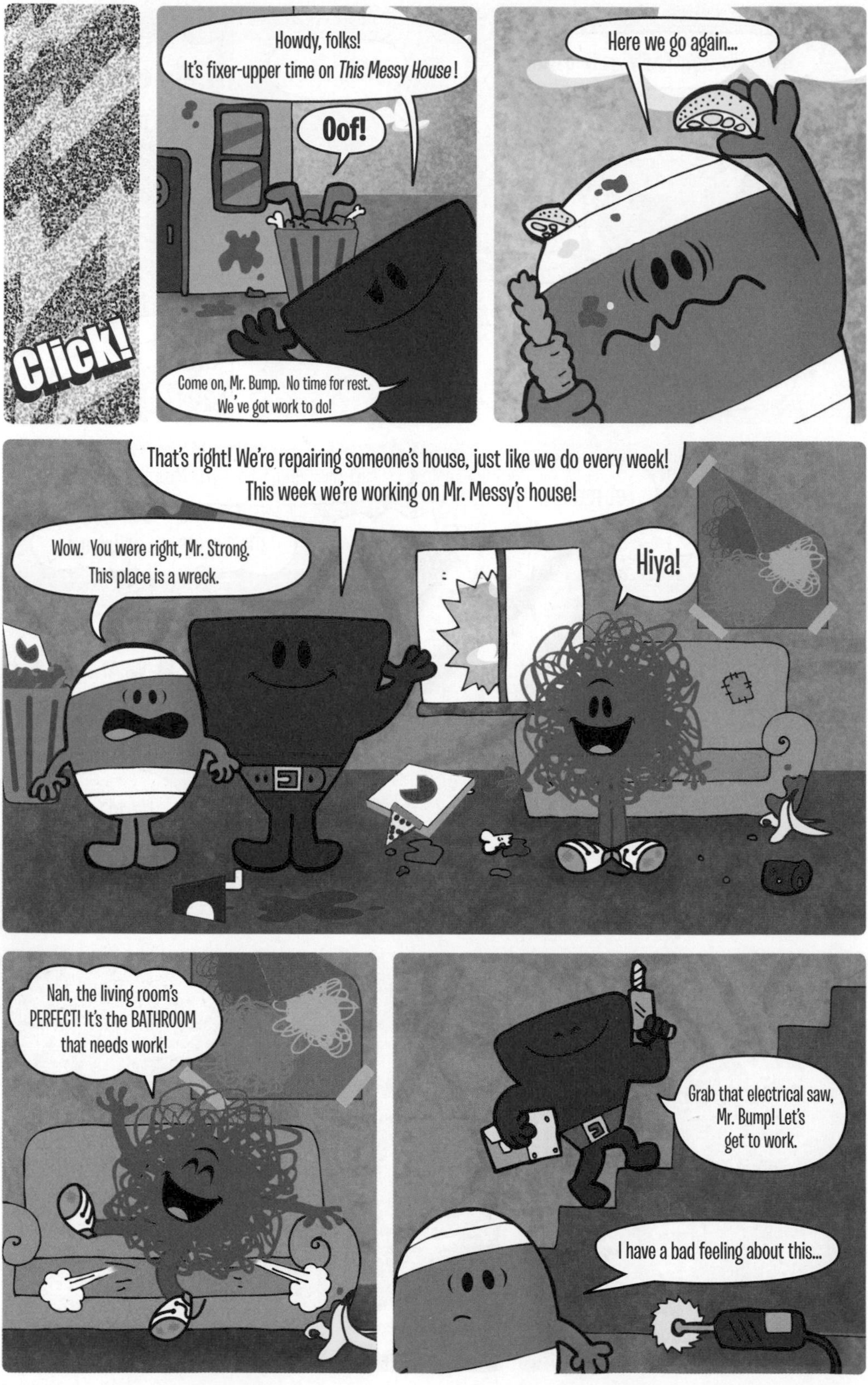
Click!
Howdy, folks!
It's fixer-upper time on *This Messy House*!
Oof!
Come on, Mr. Bump. No time for rest. We've got work to do!
Here we go again...
That's right! We're repairing someone's house, just like we do every week! This week we're working on Mr. Messy's house!
Wow. You were right, Mr. Strong. This place is a wreck.
Hiya!
Nah, the living room's PERFECT! It's the BATHROOM that needs work!
Grab that electrical saw, Mr. Bump! Let's get to work.
I have a bad feeling about this...

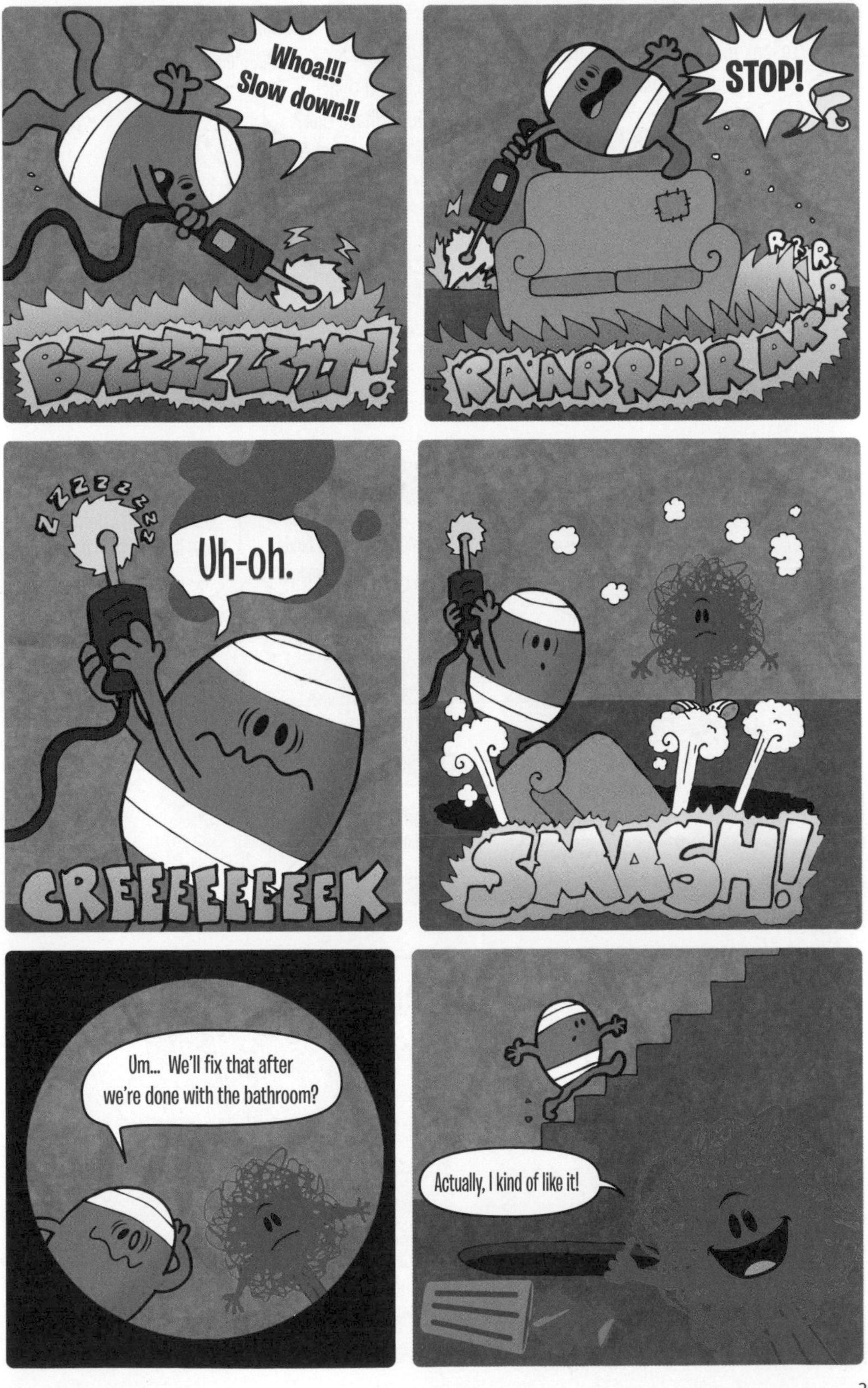
Whoa!!! Slow down!!
BZZZZZZZZZT!
STOP!
RAARRRRRAR
Uh-oh.
CREEEEEEEEK
SMASH!
Um... We'll fix that after we're done with the bathroom?
Actually, I kind of like it!

Before we get started, Mr. Bump, we need to look for the hidden dangers found in every bathroom.
Dangers?
Like slippery wet floors. Good thing Mr. Messy's floors are dry!
Good thing! Ooh. What's that?
Is it a puddle? Should I dry it up?
Oh no. It's worse. MUCH worse.
WORSE?!?
THAT, my friend, is MOLD, the MOST hidden bathroom danger.
It doesn't seem to be hiding to me.
It CREEPS into the walls and floors and, before you know it, the whole bathroom is **infested!**
Really? It doesn't look that bad. It's just a little spot.
Ahhhh!
!!!!\\\\!!!!!\\\\!!!!!!!!!*
*Release the spores!

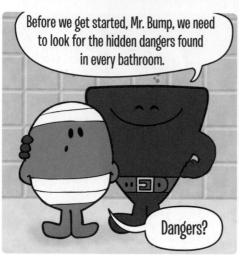

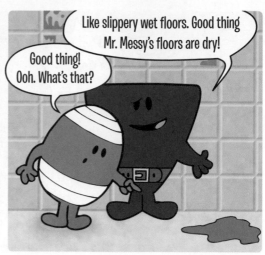

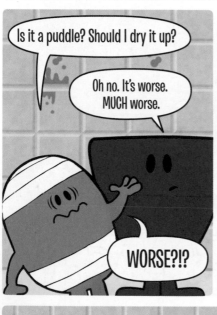

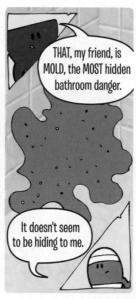

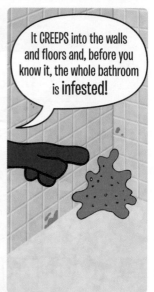

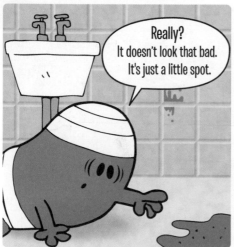

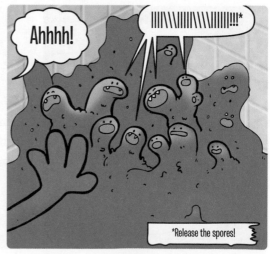

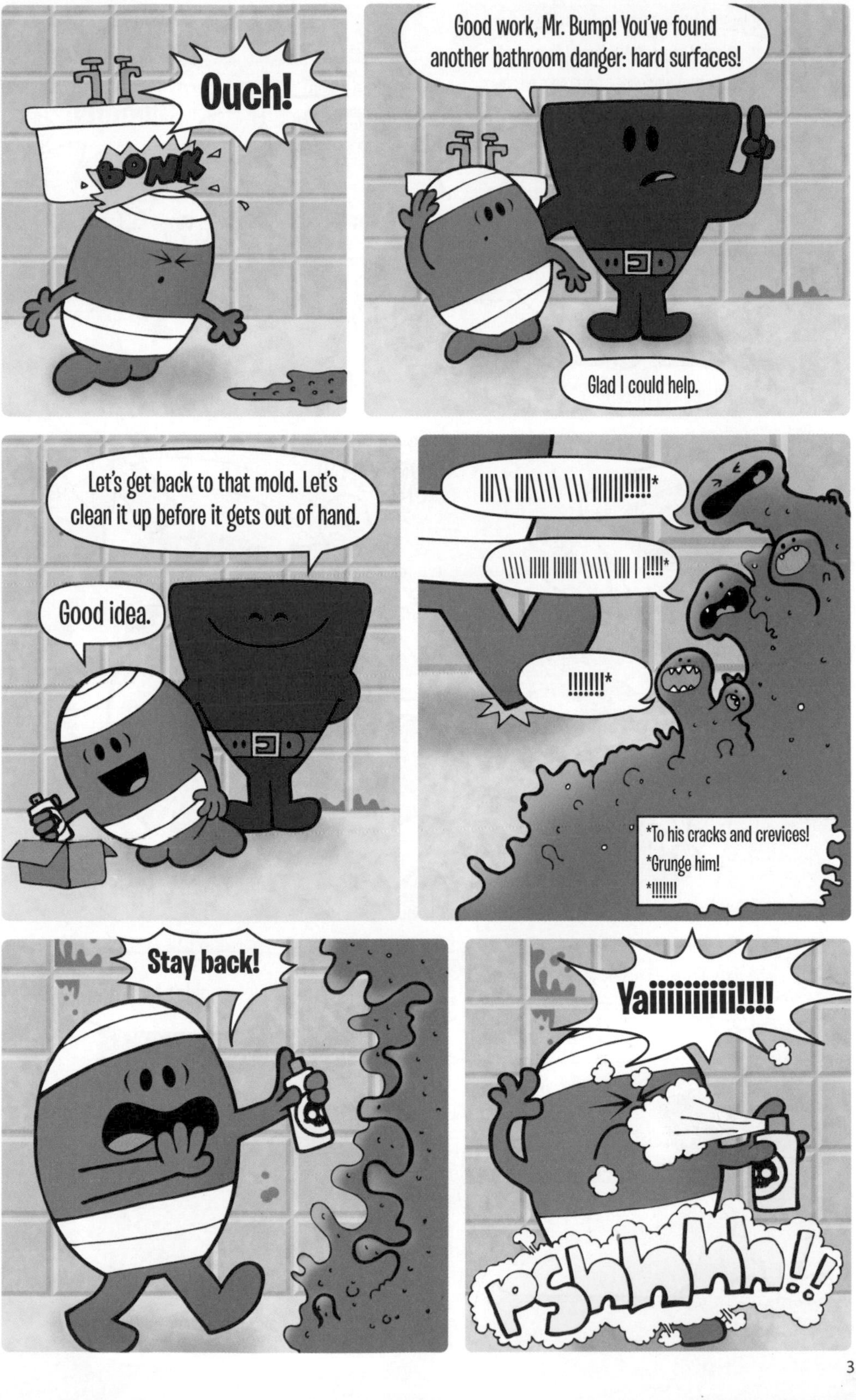
Ouch!
BONK
Good work, Mr. Bump! You've found another bathroom danger: hard surfaces!
Glad I could help.
Let's get back to that mold. Let's clean it up before it gets out of hand.
Good idea.
|||\\ ||\\\\\ \\\ |||||!!!!!*
\\\\ |||| ||||| \\\\\ ||| | |!!!!*
!!!!!!!*
*To his cracks and crevices!
*Grunge him!
*!!!!!!!
Stay back!
Yaiiiiiiiiii!!!!
PSHHHHH!!!

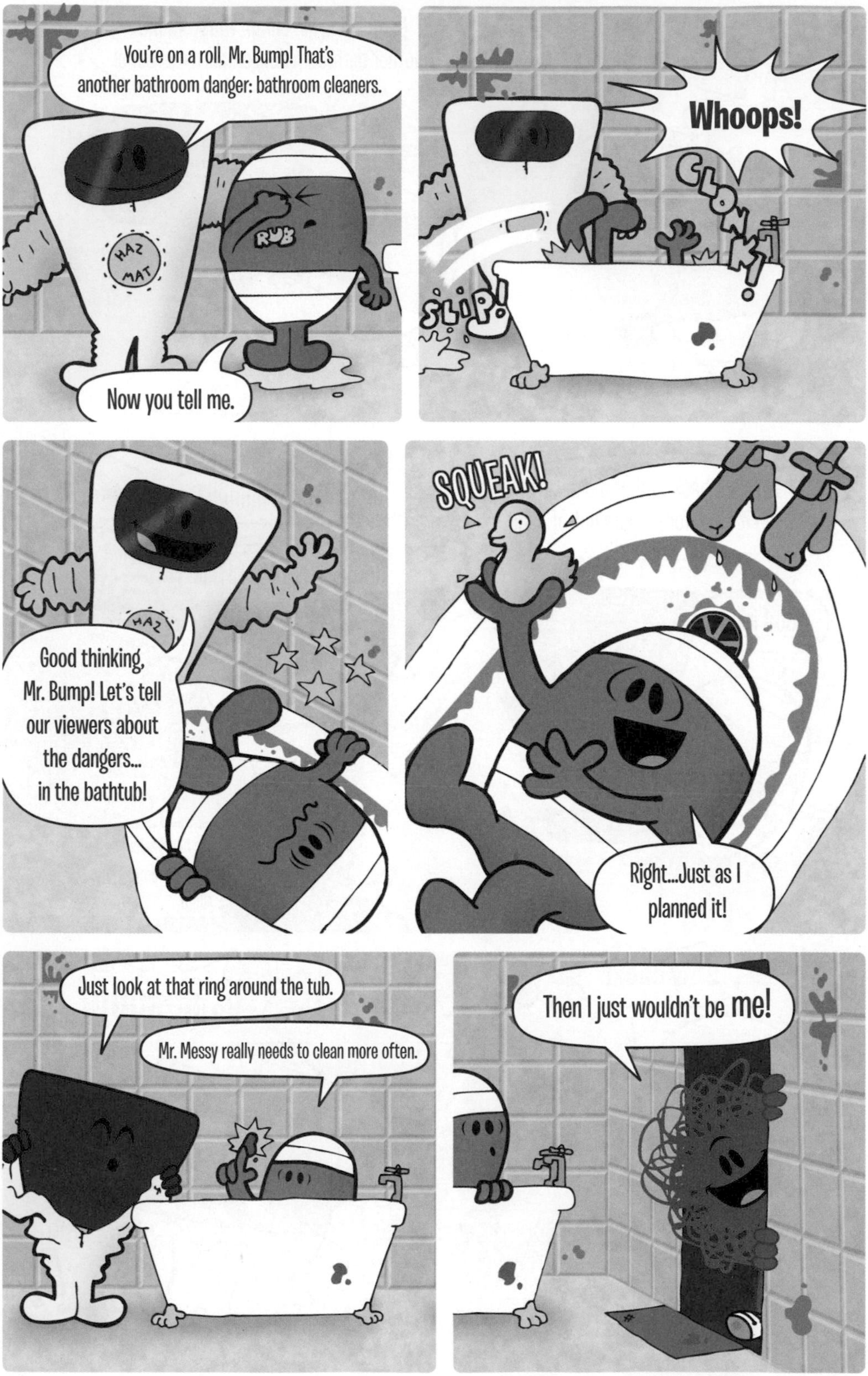

You're on a roll, Mr. Bump! That's another bathroom danger: bathroom cleaners.
HAZ MAT
RUB
Now you tell me.
Whoops!
CLONK!
SLIP!
HAZ
Good thinking, Mr. Bump! Let's tell our viewers about the dangers... in the bathtub!
SQUEAK!
Right...Just as I planned it!
Just look at that ring around the tub.
Mr. Messy really needs to clean more often.
Then I just wouldn't be me!

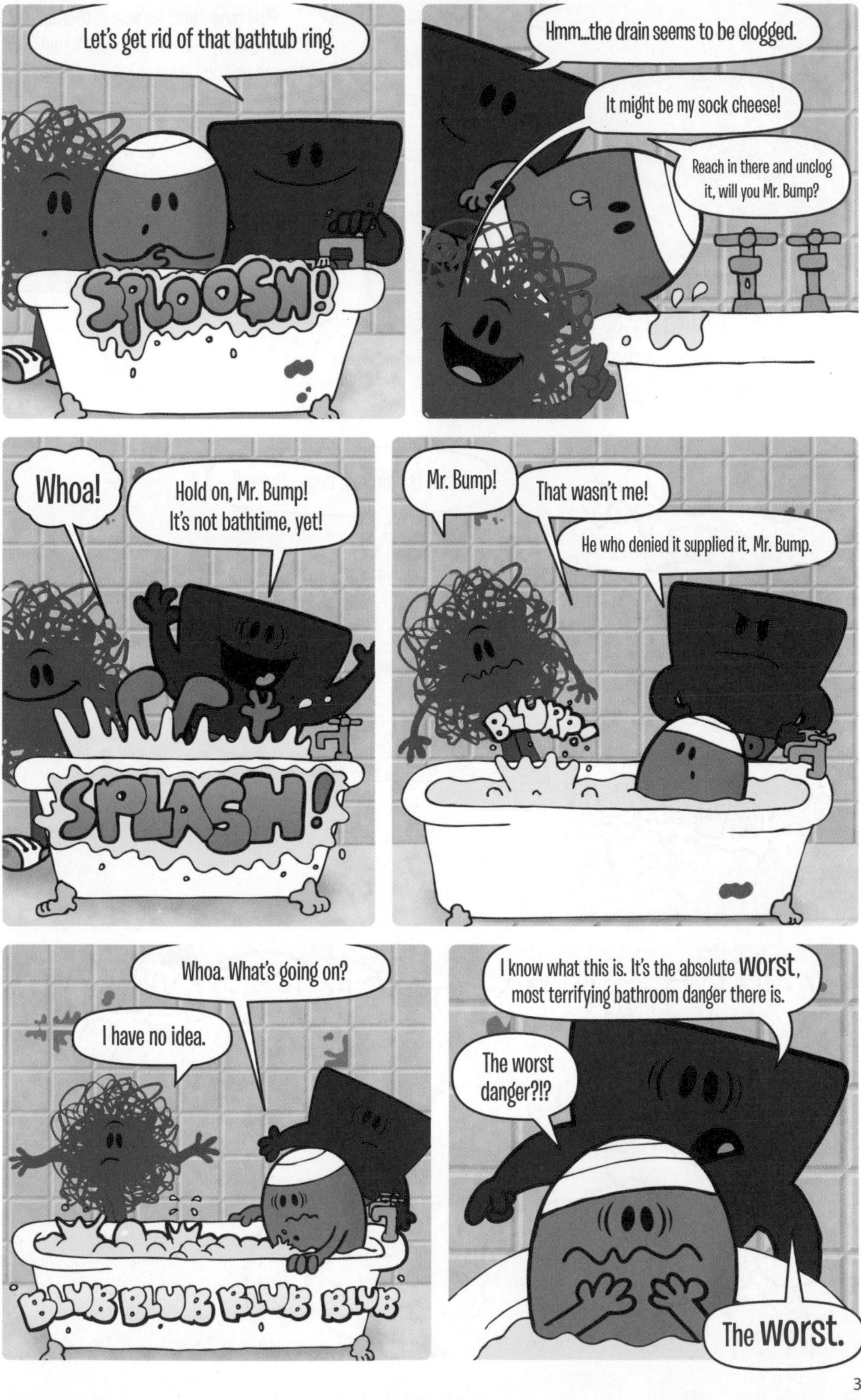
Let's get rid of that bathtub ring.
SPLOOSH!
Hmm...the drain seems to be clogged.
It might be my sock cheese!
Reach in there and unclog it, will you Mr. Bump?
Whoa!
Hold on, Mr. Bump! It's not bathtime, yet!
SPLASH!
Mr. Bump!
That wasn't me!
He who denied it supplied it, Mr. Bump.
BLUPP!
Whoa. What's going on?
I have no idea.
BLUB BLUB BLUB BLUB
I know what this is. It's the absolute worst, most terrifying bathroom danger there is.
The worst danger?!?
The worst.

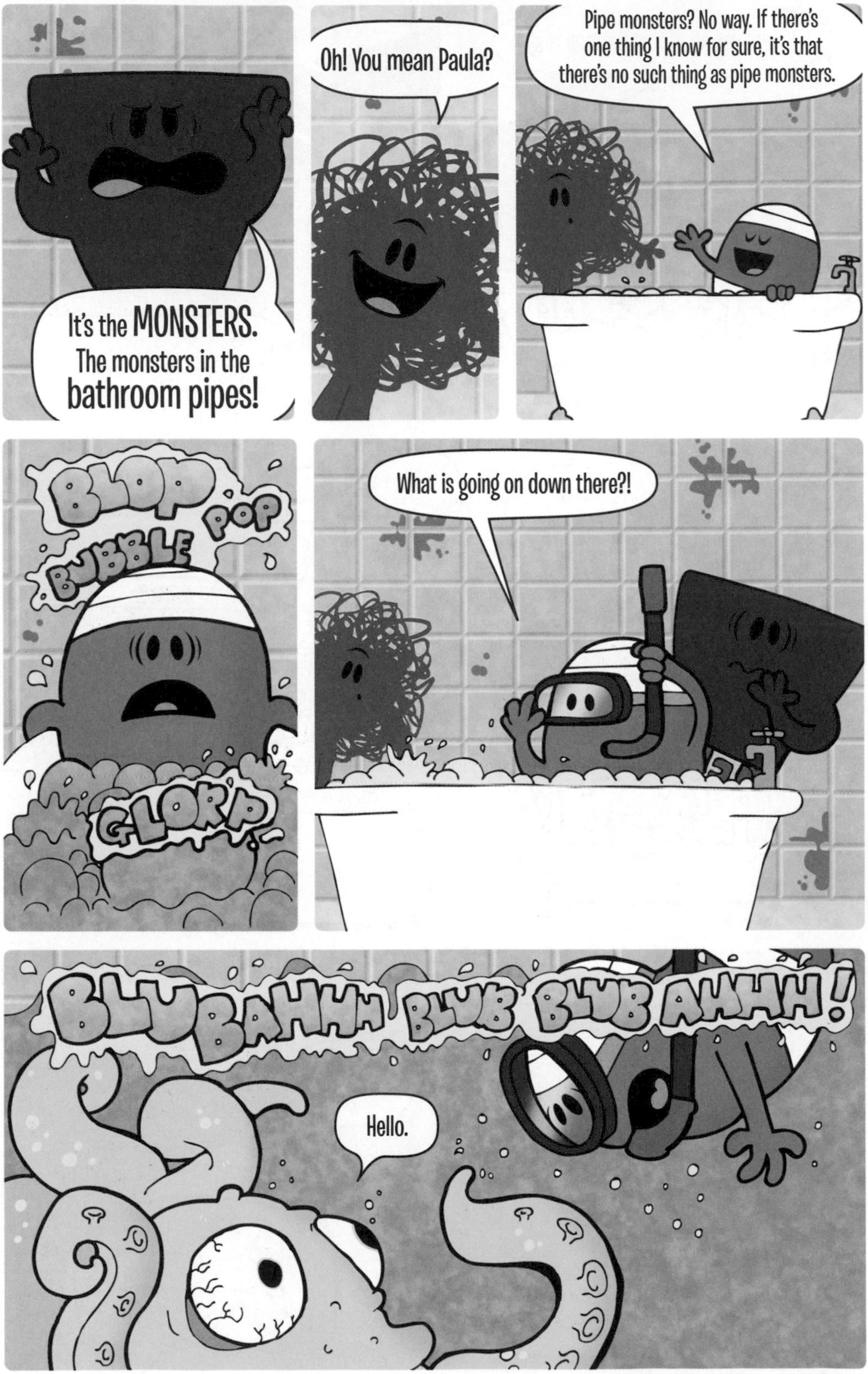
It's the MONSTERS. The monsters in the bathroom pipes!
Oh! You mean Paula?
Pipe monsters? No way. If there's one thing I know for sure, it's that there's no such thing as pipe monsters.
BLOP
BUBBLE POP
GLORP!
What is going on down there?!
BLUBAHHH BLUB BLUB AHHH!
Hello.

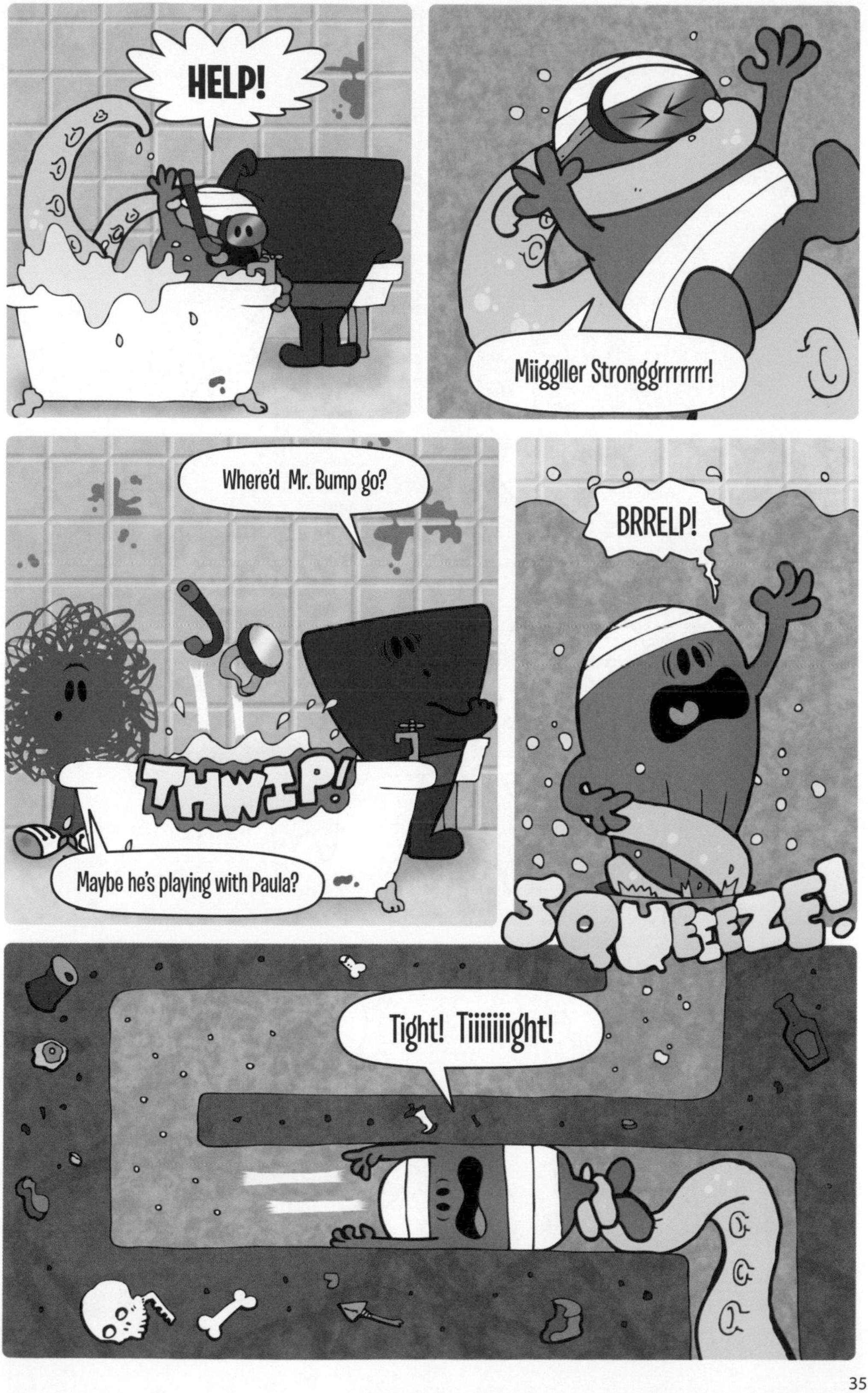
HELP!
Miiggller Stronggrrrrrrr!
Where'd Mr. Bump go?
THWIP!
Maybe he's playing with Paula?
BRRELP!
SQUEEEZE!
Tight! Tiiiiiiight!

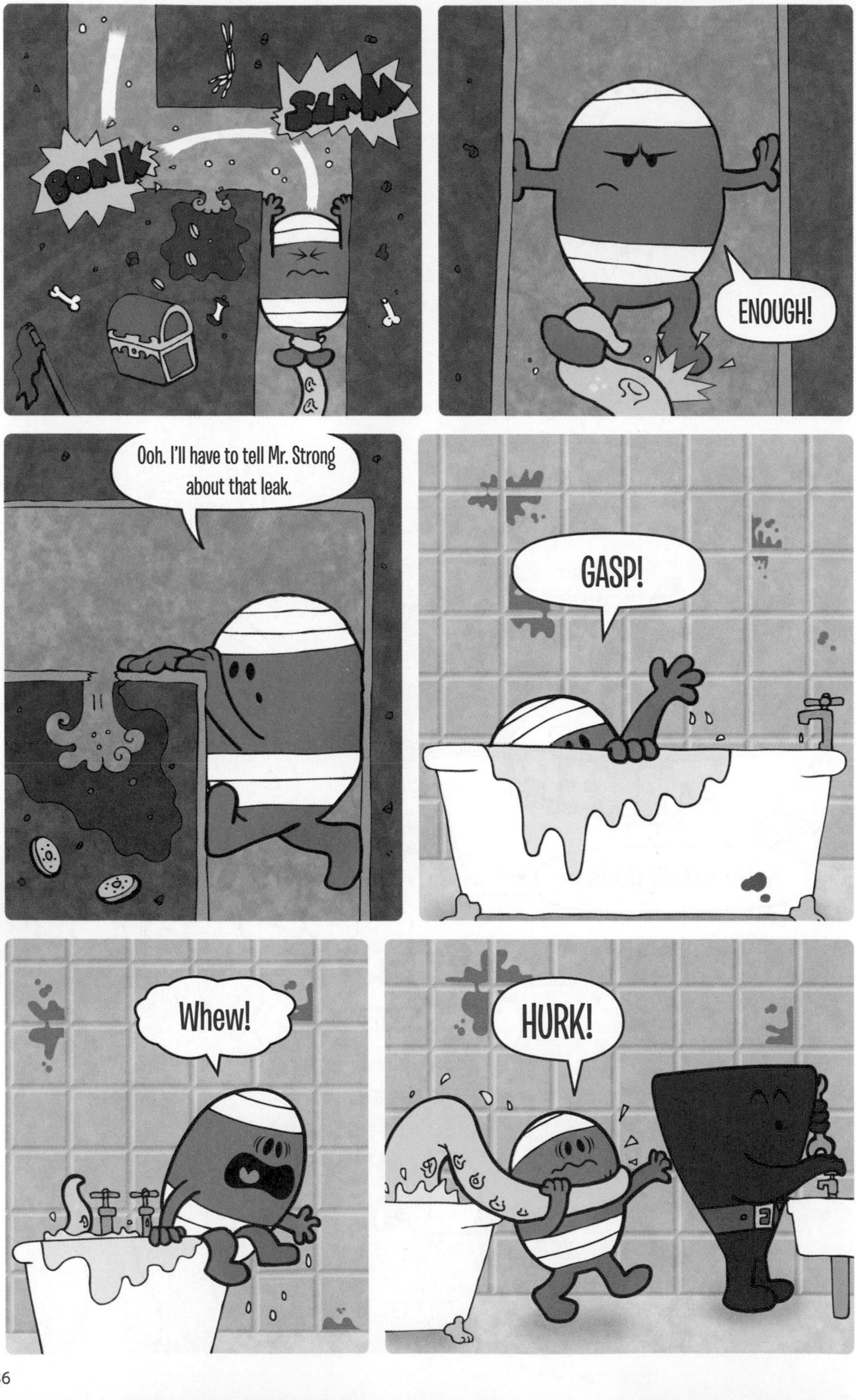
BONK
SLAM
ENOUGH!
Ooh. I'll have to tell Mr. Strong about that leak.
GASP!
Whew!
HURK!

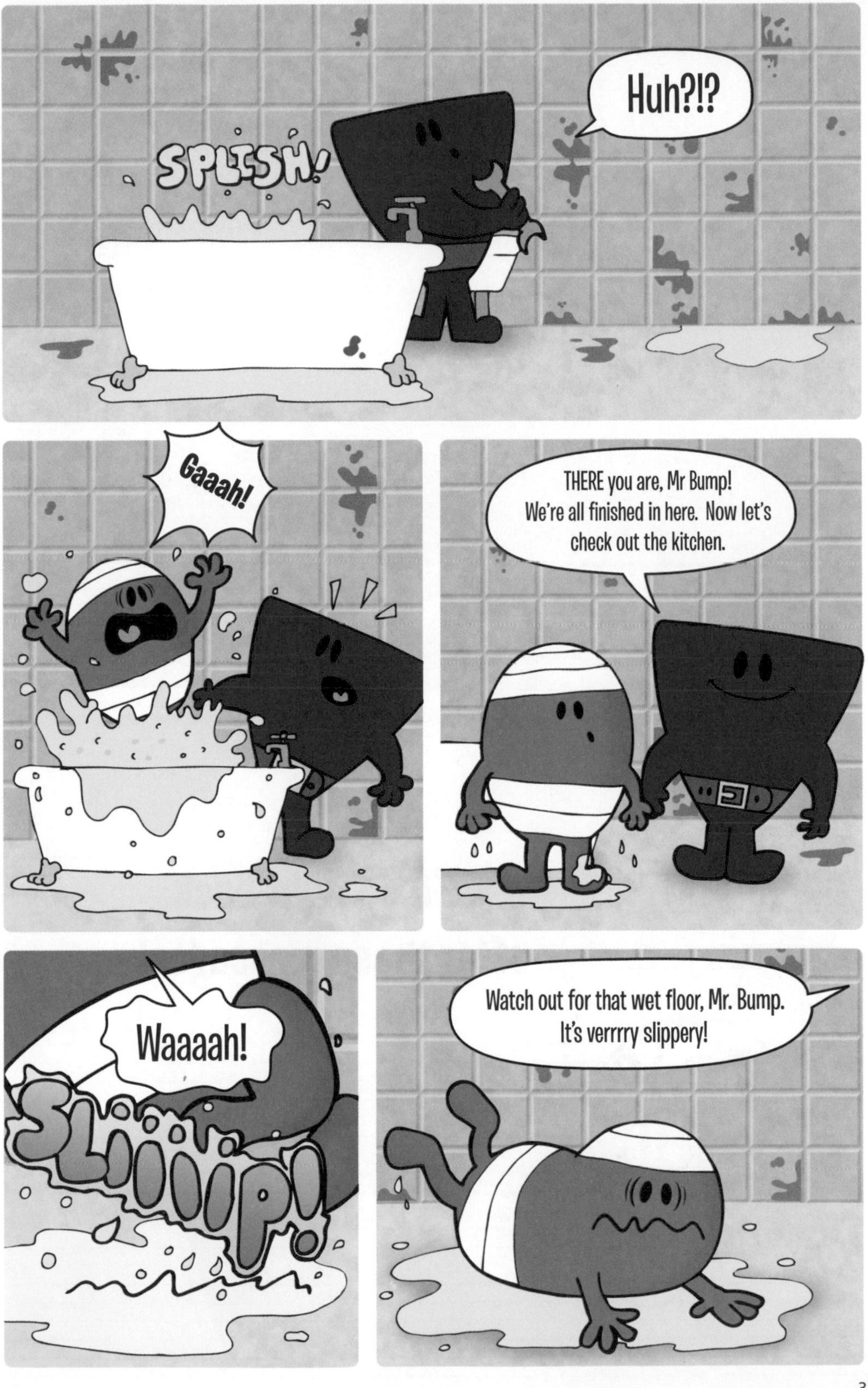
SPLISH!
Huh?!?
Gaaah!
THERE you are, Mr Bump! We're all finished in here. Now let's check out the kitchen.
Waaaah!
SLIIIIP!
Watch out for that wet floor, Mr. Bump. It's verrrry slippery!

We'll be right back
after these messages!

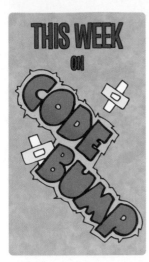

THIS WEEK ON CODE BUMP

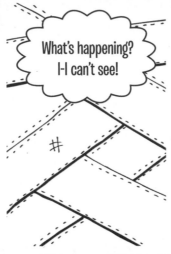

What's happening? I-I can't see!

Relax, Mr. Bump. You came through surgery just fine!

Surgery?!

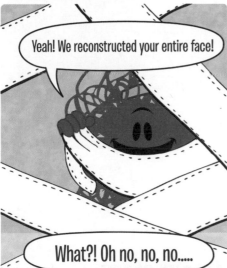

Yeah! We reconstructed your entire face!

What?! Oh no, no, no.....

Shazam that's good!

Lemmesee! Lemmesee!!

Poopity poop!

Now back to our story...

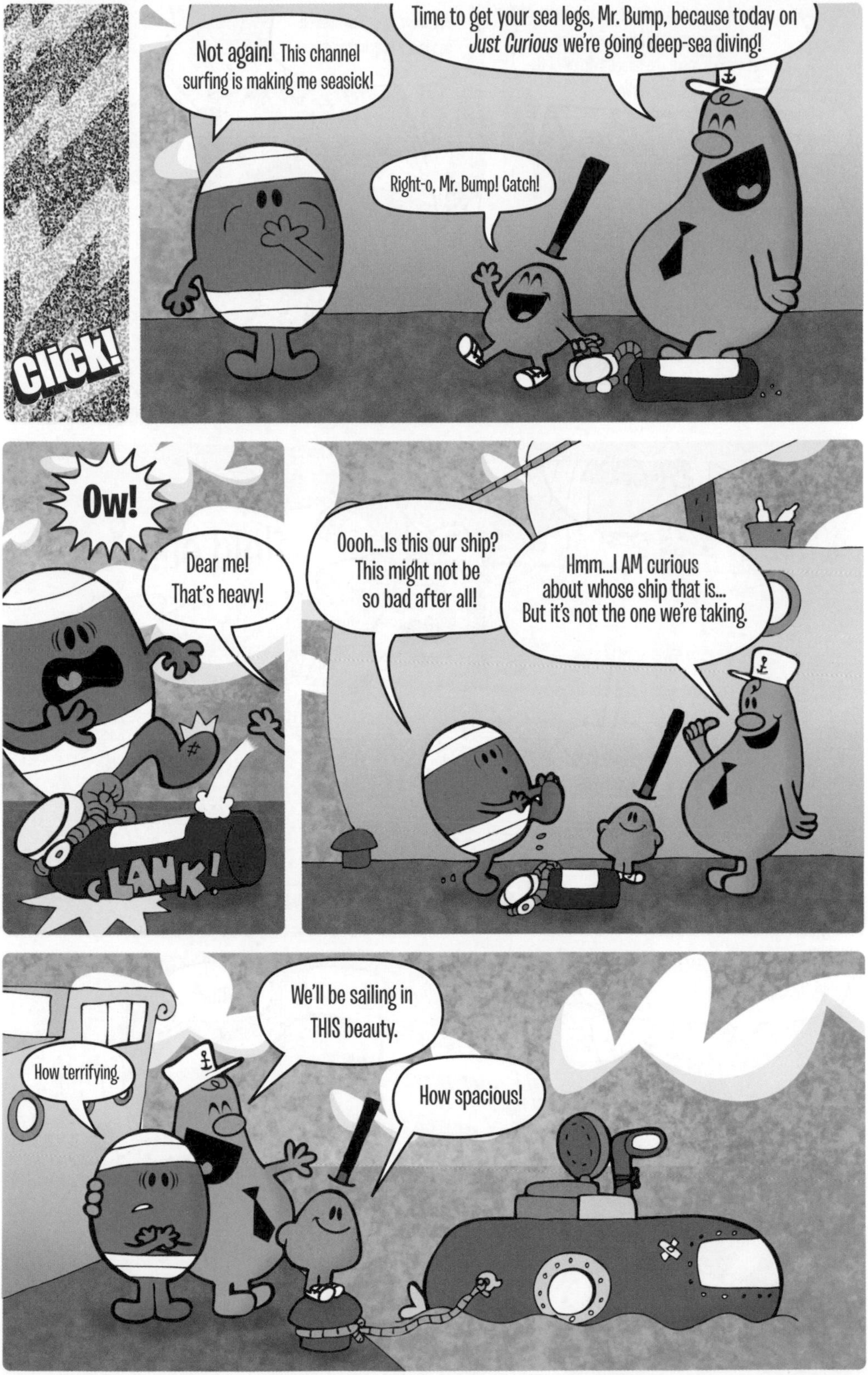
Click!
Not again! This channel surfing is making me seasick!
Time to get your sea legs, Mr. Bump, because today on *Just Curious* we're going deep-sea diving!
Right-o, Mr. Bump! Catch!
Ow!
Dear me! That's heavy!
CLANK!
Oooh...Is this our ship? This might not be so bad after all!
Hmm...I AM curious about whose ship that is... But it's not the one we're taking.
How terrifying.
We'll be sailing in THIS beauty.
How spacious!

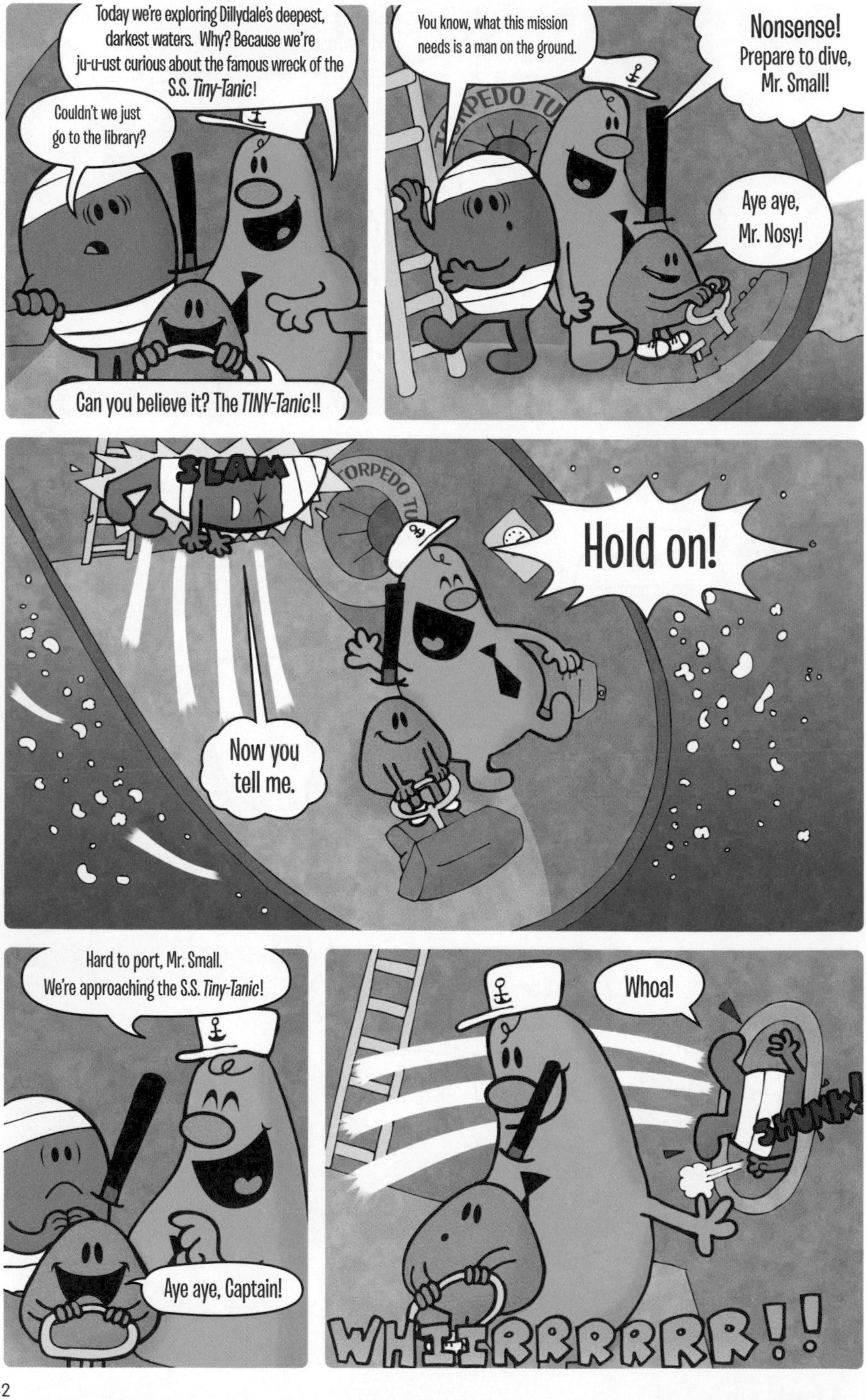

Today we're exploring Dillydale's deepest, darkest waters. Why? Because we're ju-u-ust curious about the famous wreck of the S.S. *Tiny-Tanic*!
Couldn't we just go to the library?
Can you believe it? The *TINY-Tanic*!!
You know, what this mission needs is a man on the ground.
TORPEDO TU
Nonsense! Prepare to dive, Mr. Small!
Aye aye, Mr. Nosy!
SLAM
TORPEDO TU
Hold on!
Now you tell me.
Hard to port, Mr. Small. We're approaching the S.S. *Tiny-Tanic*!
Aye aye, Captain!
Whoa!
SHUNK!
WHIRRRRRR!!

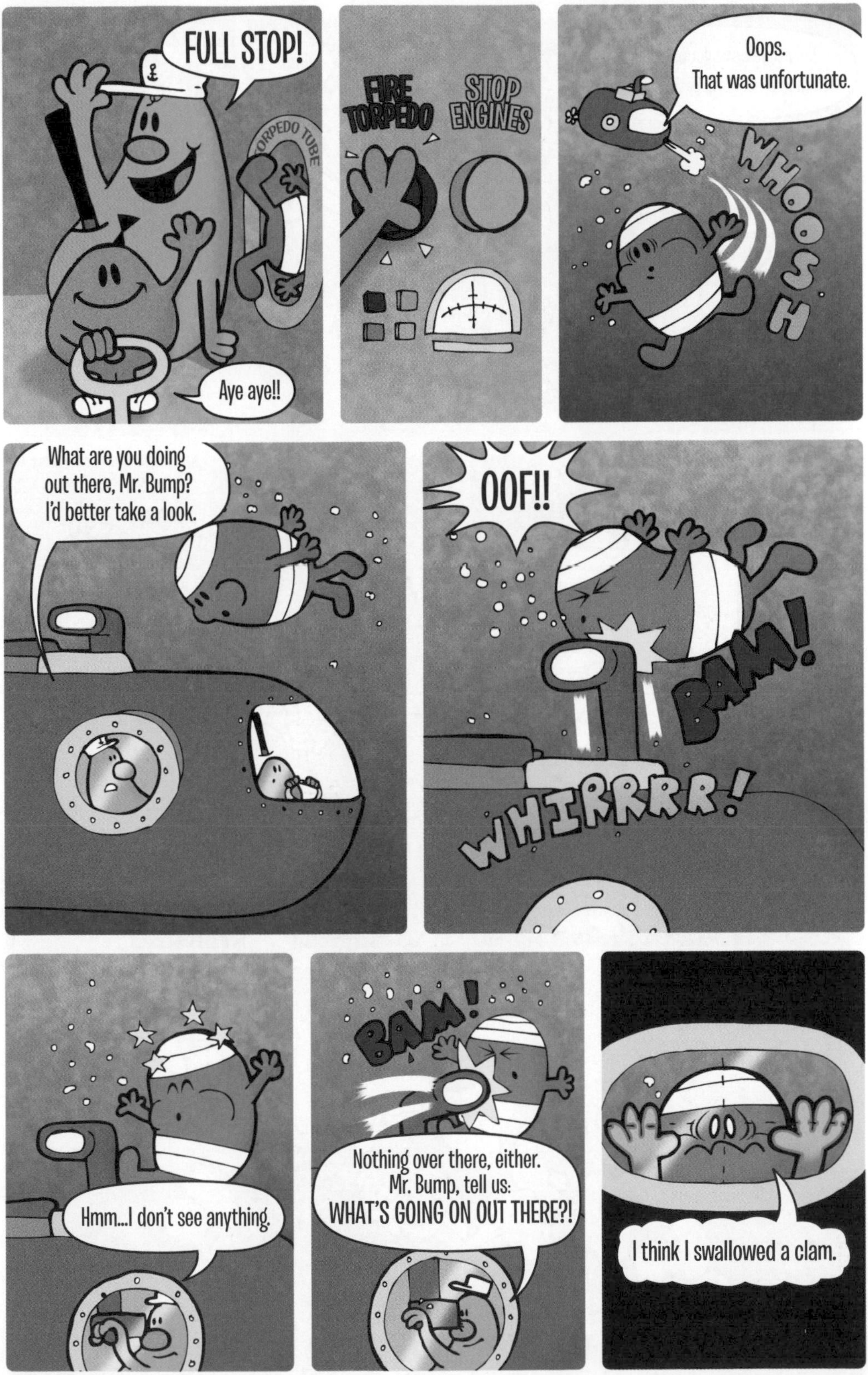
FULL STOP!
TORPEDO TUBE
Aye aye!!
FIRE TORPEDO
STOP ENGINES
Oops.
That was unfortunate.
WHOOSH
What are you doing out there, Mr. Bump? I'd better take a look.
OOF!!
BAM!
WHIRRRR!
Hmm...I don't see anything.
BAM!
Nothing over there, either.
Mr. Bump, tell us:
WHAT'S GOING ON OUT THERE?!
I think I swallowed a clam.

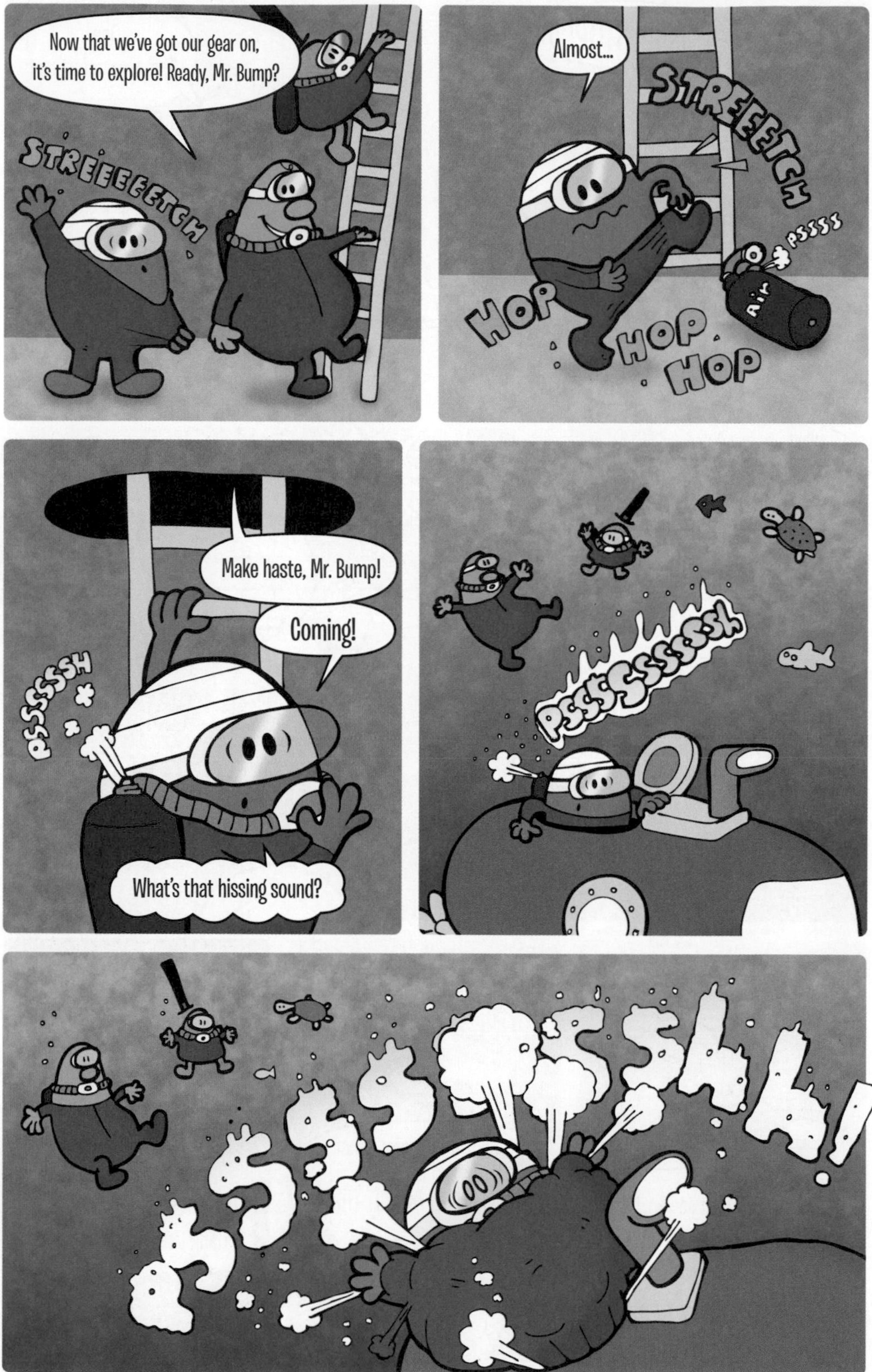
Now that we've got our gear on, it's time to explore! Ready, Mr. Bump?
STREEEEEETCH
Almost...
STREEEETCH
PSSSS
Air
HOP
HOP
HOP
Make haste, Mr. Bump!
Coming!
PSSSSSH
What's that hissing sound?
PSSSSSSSSSH
SSSSSSHH!

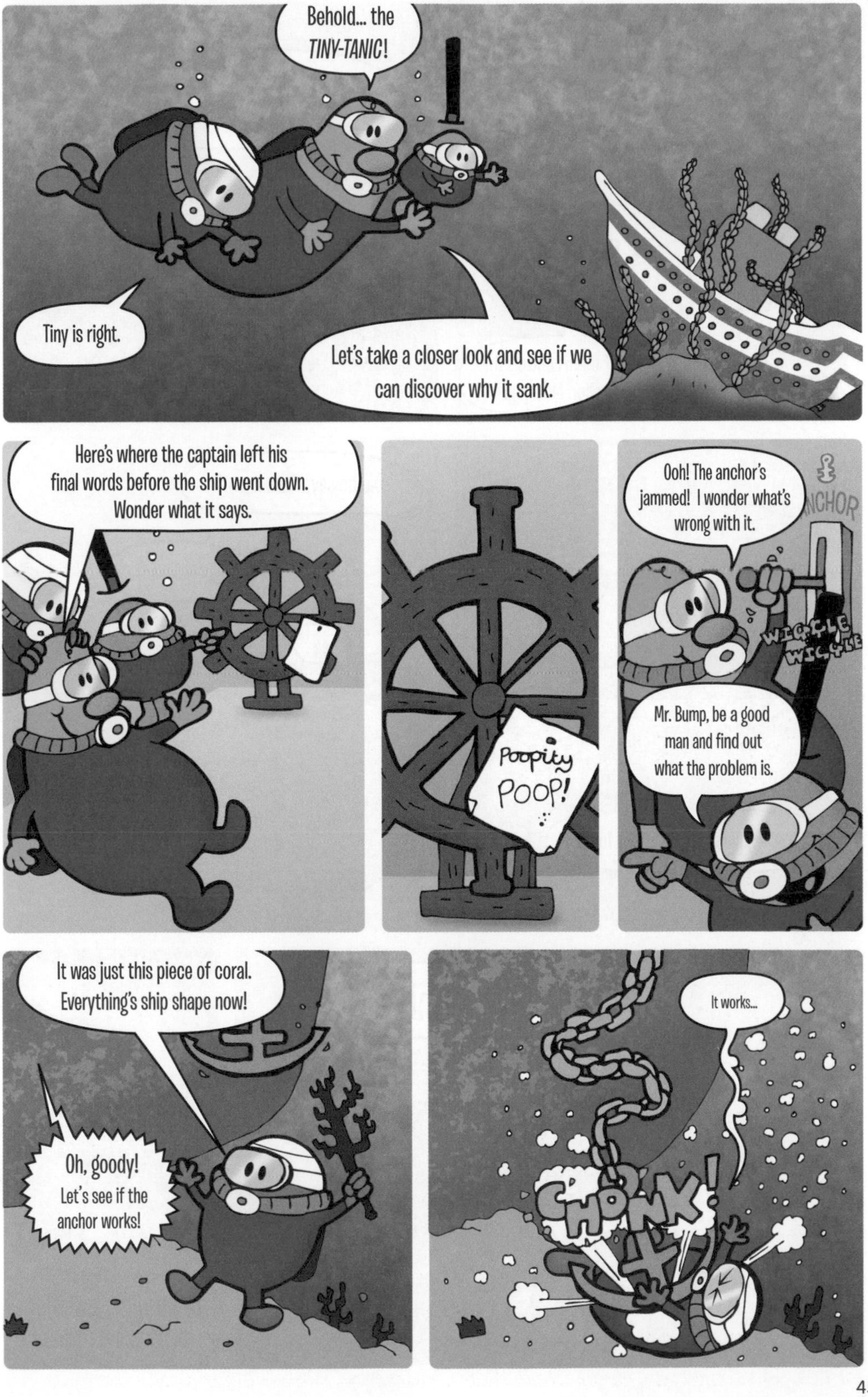
Behold... the *TINY-TANIC*!
Tiny is right.
Let's take a closer look and see if we can discover why it sank.
Here's where the captain left his final words before the ship went down. Wonder what it says.
Poopity POOP!
Ooh! The anchor's jammed! I wonder what's wrong with it.
NCHOR
WIGGLE WIGGLE
Mr. Bump, be a good man and find out what the problem is.
It was just this piece of coral. Everything's ship shape now!
Oh, goody! Let's see if the anchor works!
It works...
CHONK!

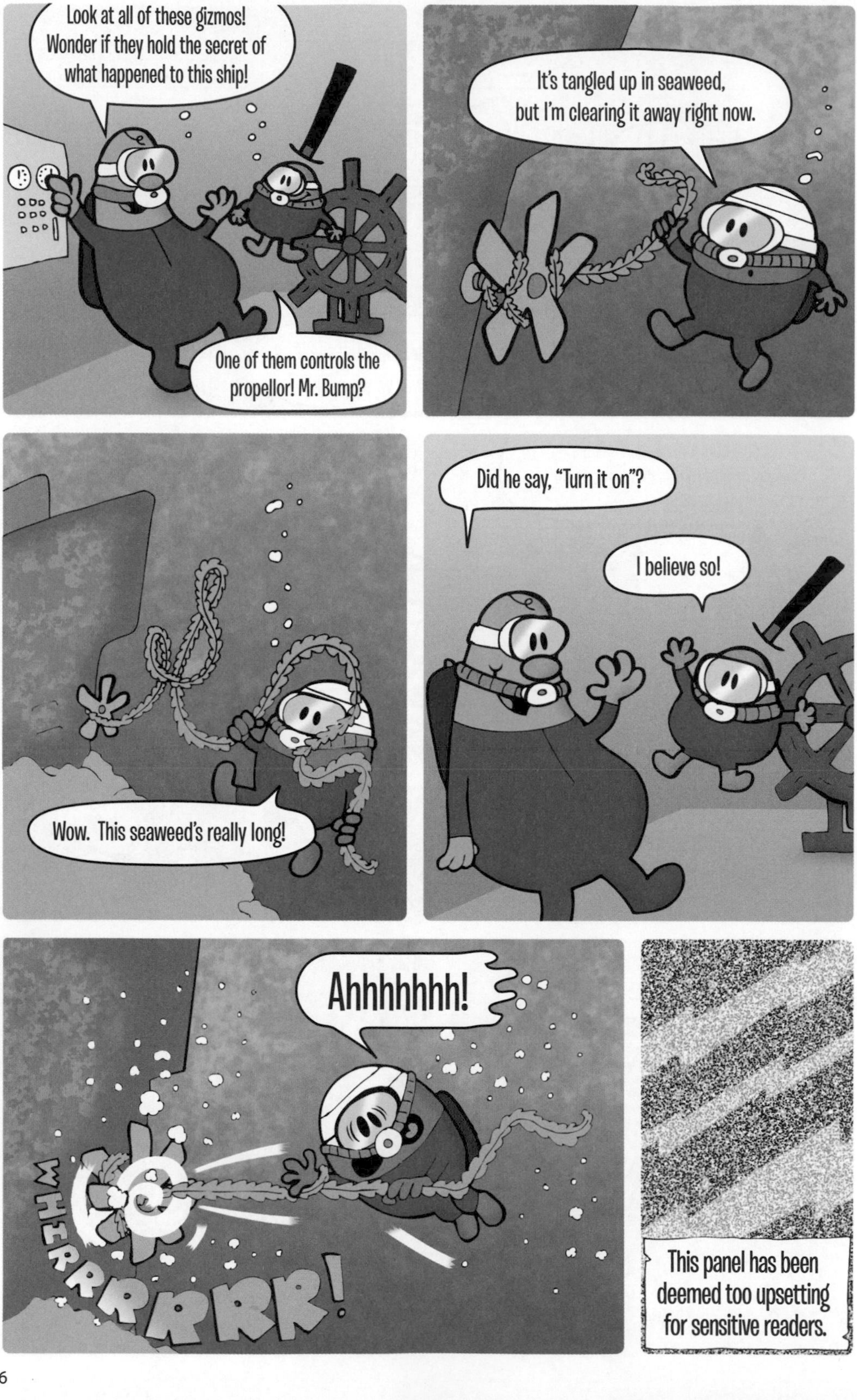
Look at all of these gizmos! Wonder if they hold the secret of what happened to this ship!
One of them controls the propellor! Mr. Bump?
It's tangled up in seaweed, but I'm clearing it away right now.
Wow. This seaweed's really long!
Did he say, "Turn it on"?
I believe so!
Ahhhhhhh!
WHIRRRRRR!
This panel has been deemed too upsetting for sensitive readers.

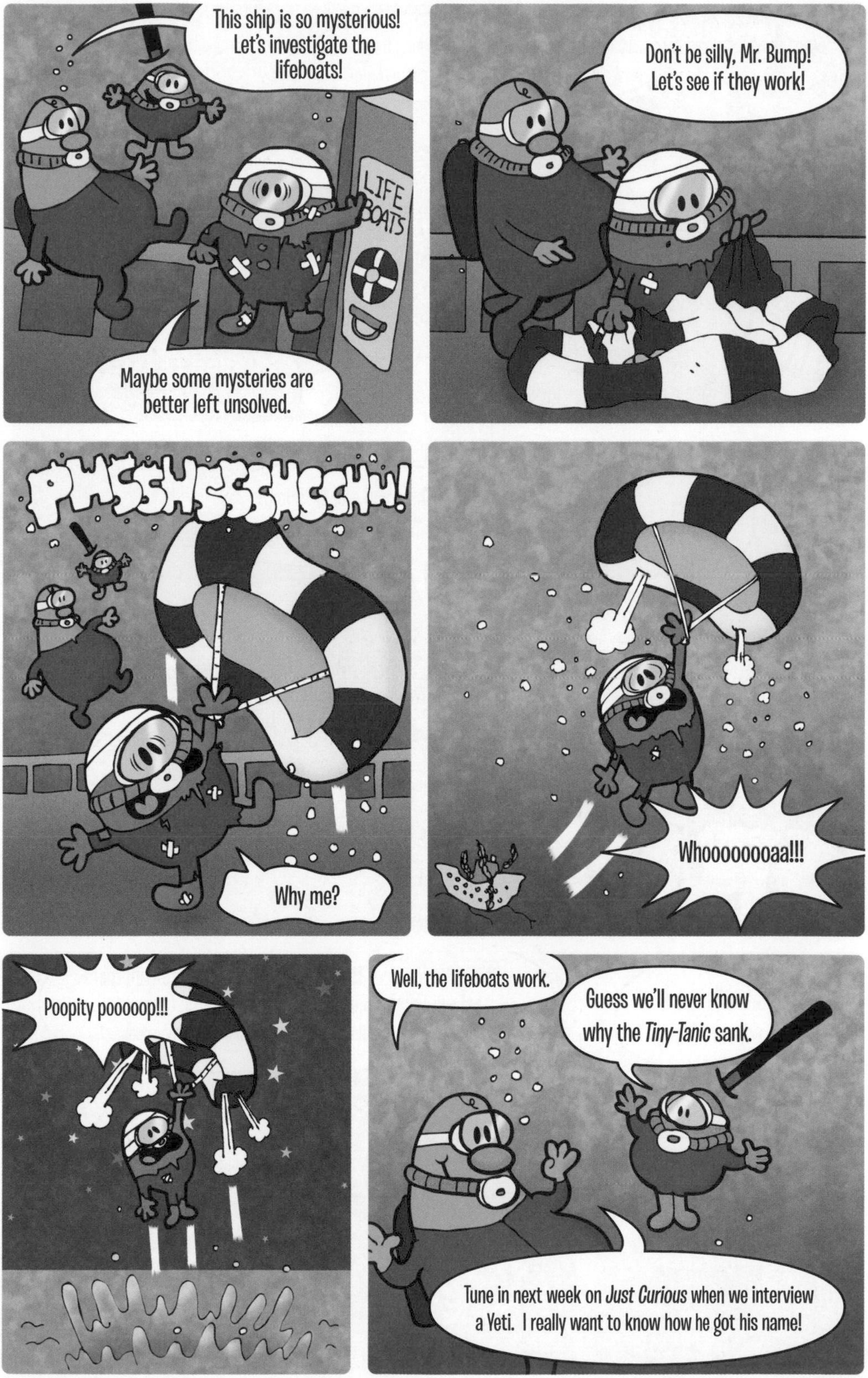
This ship is so mysterious! Let's investigate the lifeboats!
LIFE BOATS
Maybe some mysteries are better left unsolved.
Don't be silly, Mr. Bump! Let's see if they work!
PHSSHSSSHSSHH!
Why me?
Whoooooooaa!!!
Poopity poooop!!!
Well, the lifeboats work.
Guess we'll never know why the *Tiny-Tanic* sank.
Tune in next week on *Just Curious* when we interview a Yeti. I really want to know how he got his name!

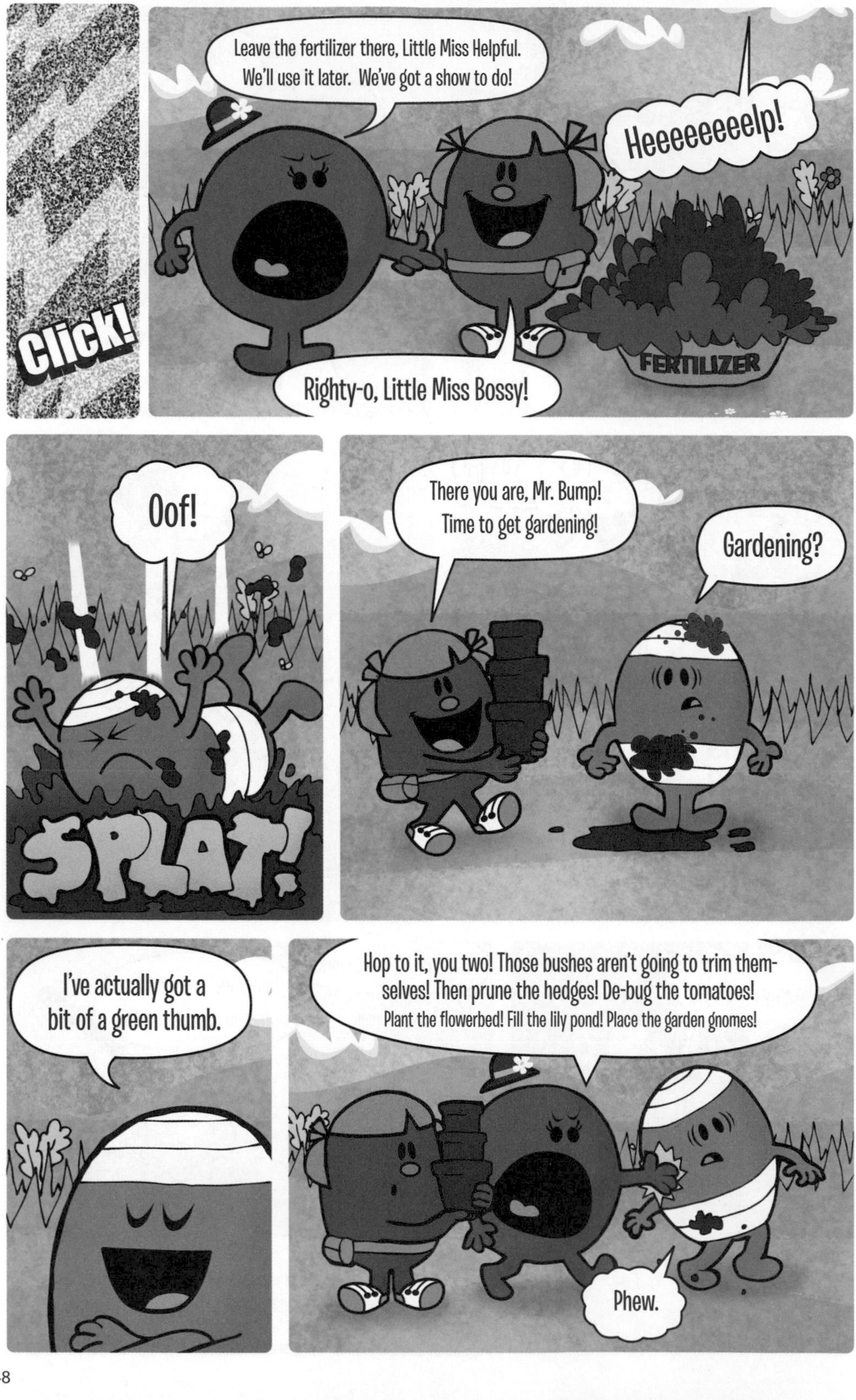
Click!
Leave the fertilizer there, Little Miss Helpful. We'll use it later. We've got a show to do!
Heeeeeeeelp!
FERTILIZER
Righty-o, Little Miss Bossy!
Oof!
SPLAT!
There you are, Mr. Bump! Time to get gardening!
Gardening?
I've actually got a bit of a green thumb.
Hop to it, you two! Those bushes aren't going to trim themselves! Then prune the hedges! De-bug the tomatoes! Plant the flowerbed! Fill the lily pond! Place the garden gnomes!
Phew.

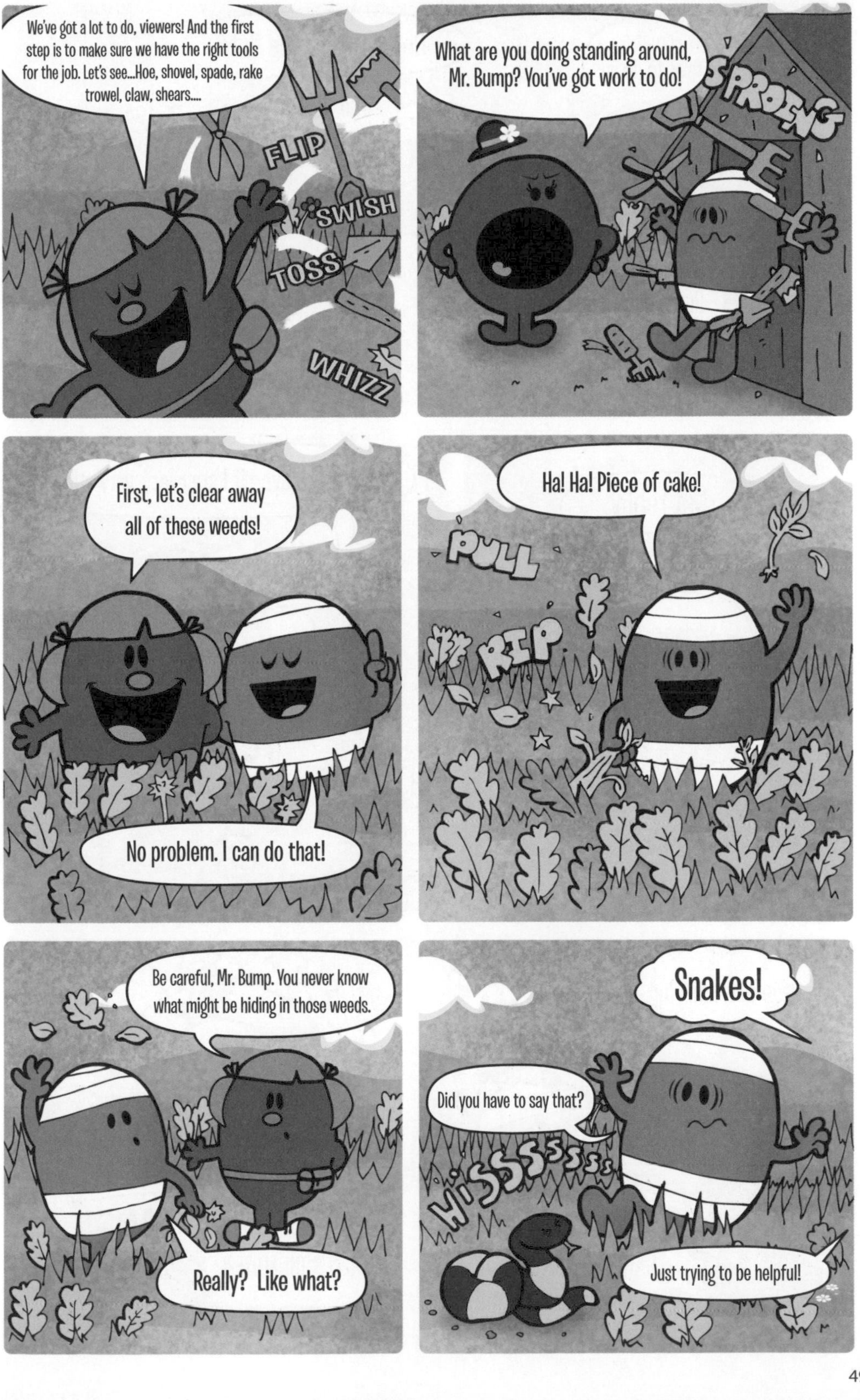
We've got a lot to do, viewers! And the first step is to make sure we have the right tools for the job. Let's see...Hoe, shovel, spade, rake trowel, claw, shears....
FLIP
SWISH
TOSS
WHIZZ
What are you doing standing around, Mr. Bump? You've got work to do!
SPROING
First, let's clear away all of these weeds!
No problem. I can do that!
Ha! Ha! Piece of cake!
PULL
RIP
Be careful, Mr. Bump. You never know what might be hiding in those weeds.
Really? Like what?
Snakes!
Did you have to say that?
HiSSSSSSS
Just trying to be helpful!

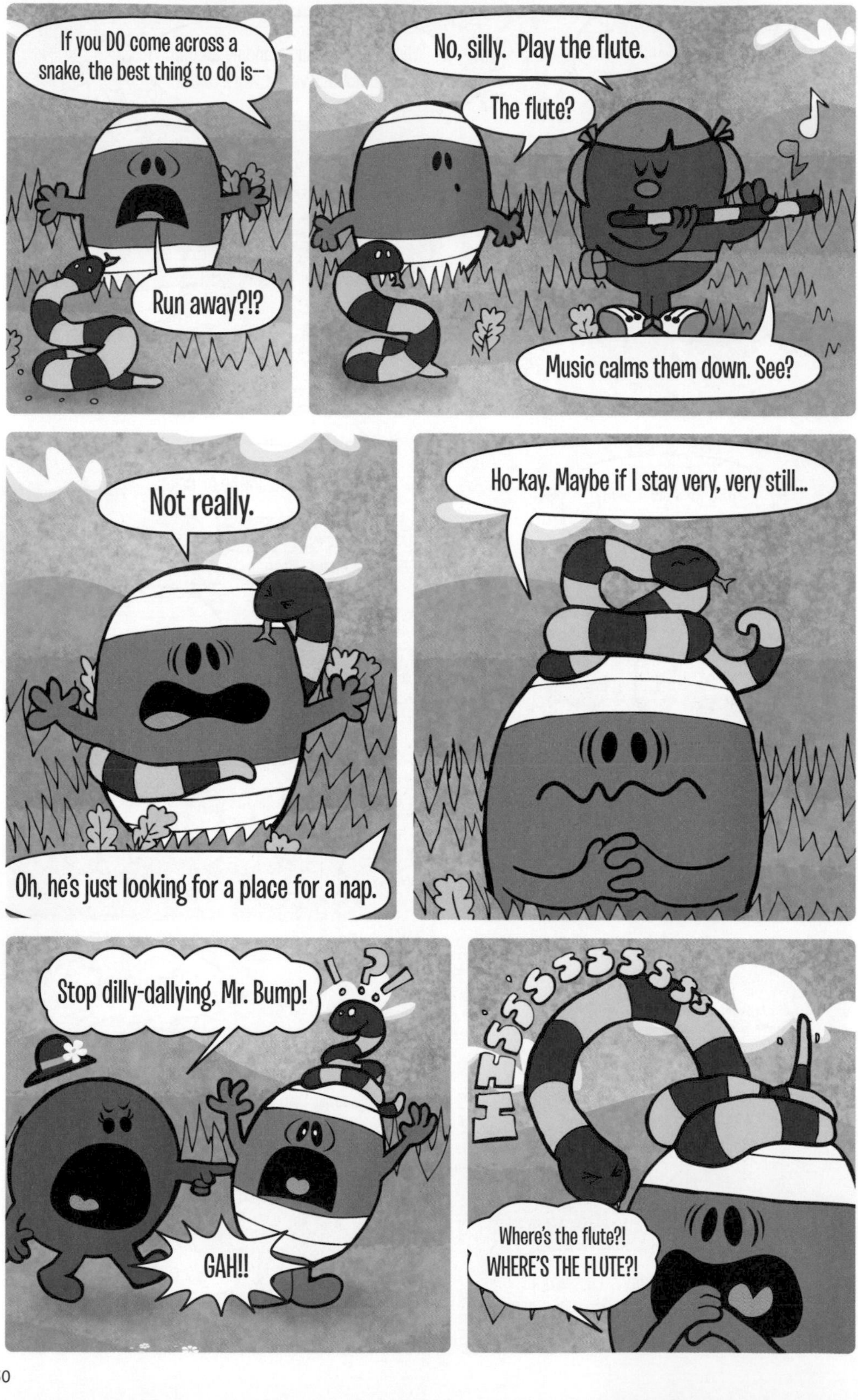
If you DO come across a snake, the best thing to do is--
Run away?!?
No, silly. Play the flute.
The flute?
Music calms them down. See?
Not really.
Oh, he's just looking for a place for a nap.
Ho-kay. Maybe if I stay very, very still...
Stop dilly-dallying, Mr. Bump!
GAH!!
HISSSSSSSSSS
Where's the flute?!
WHERE'S THE FLUTE?!

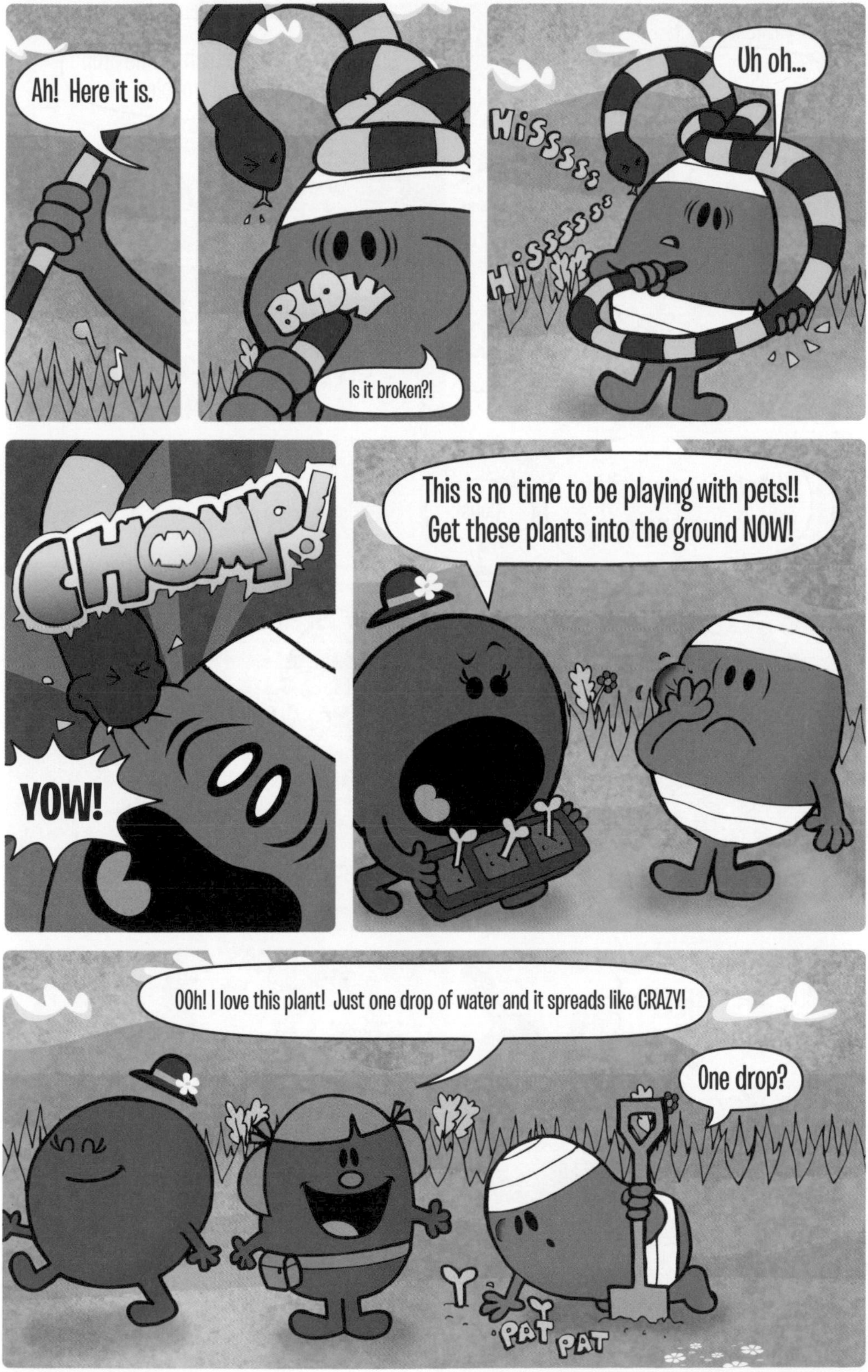
Ah! Here it is.
BLOW
Is it broken?!
HISSSSSS
HISSSSSS
Uh oh...
CHOMP!
YOW!
This is no time to be playing with pets!! Get these plants into the ground NOW!
OOh! I love this plant! Just one drop of water and it spreads like CRAZY!
One drop?
PAT PAT

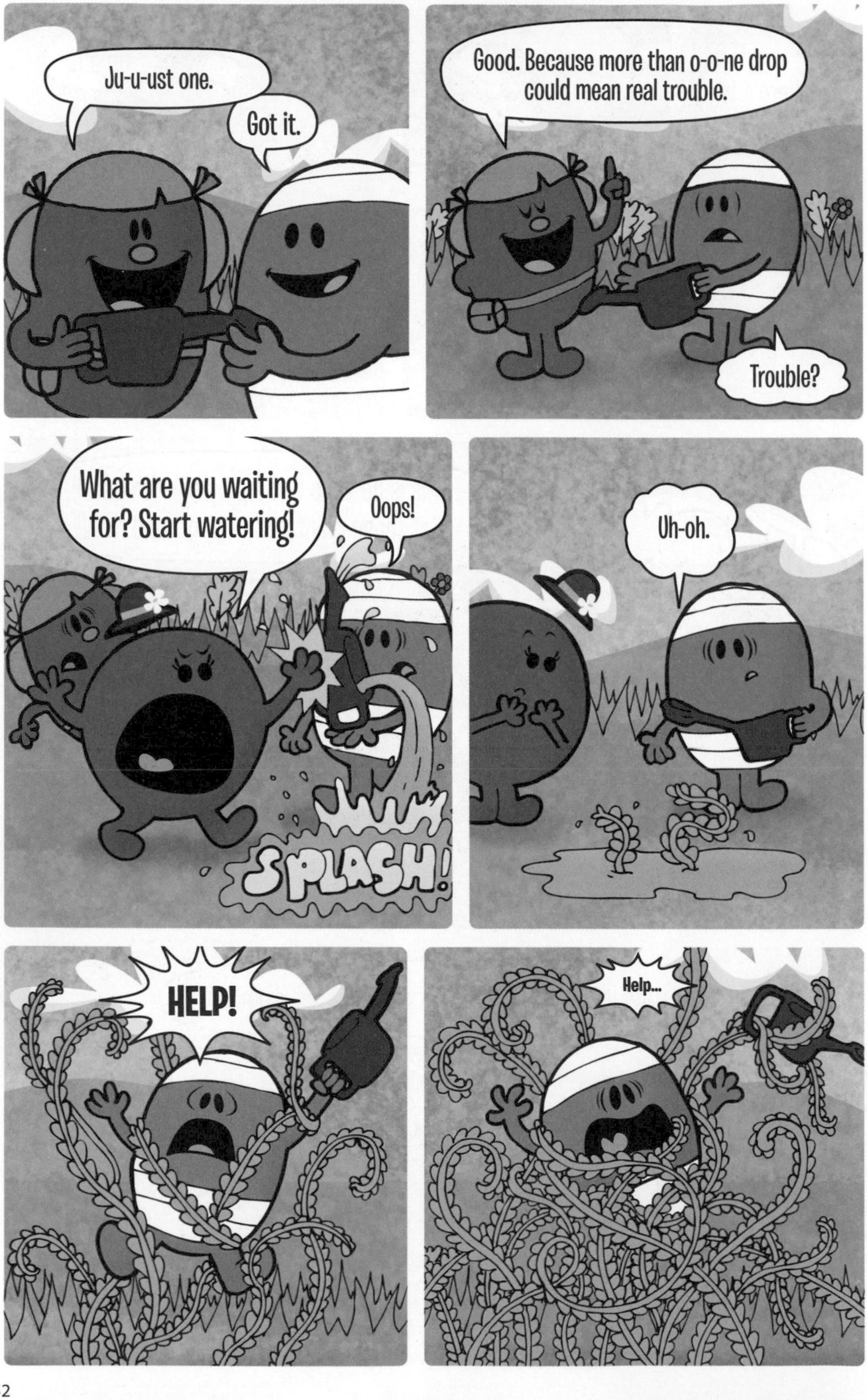
Ju-u-ust one.
Got it.
Good. Because more than o-o-ne drop could mean real trouble.
Trouble?
What are you waiting for? Start watering!
Oops!
SPLASH!
Uh-oh.
HELP!
Help...

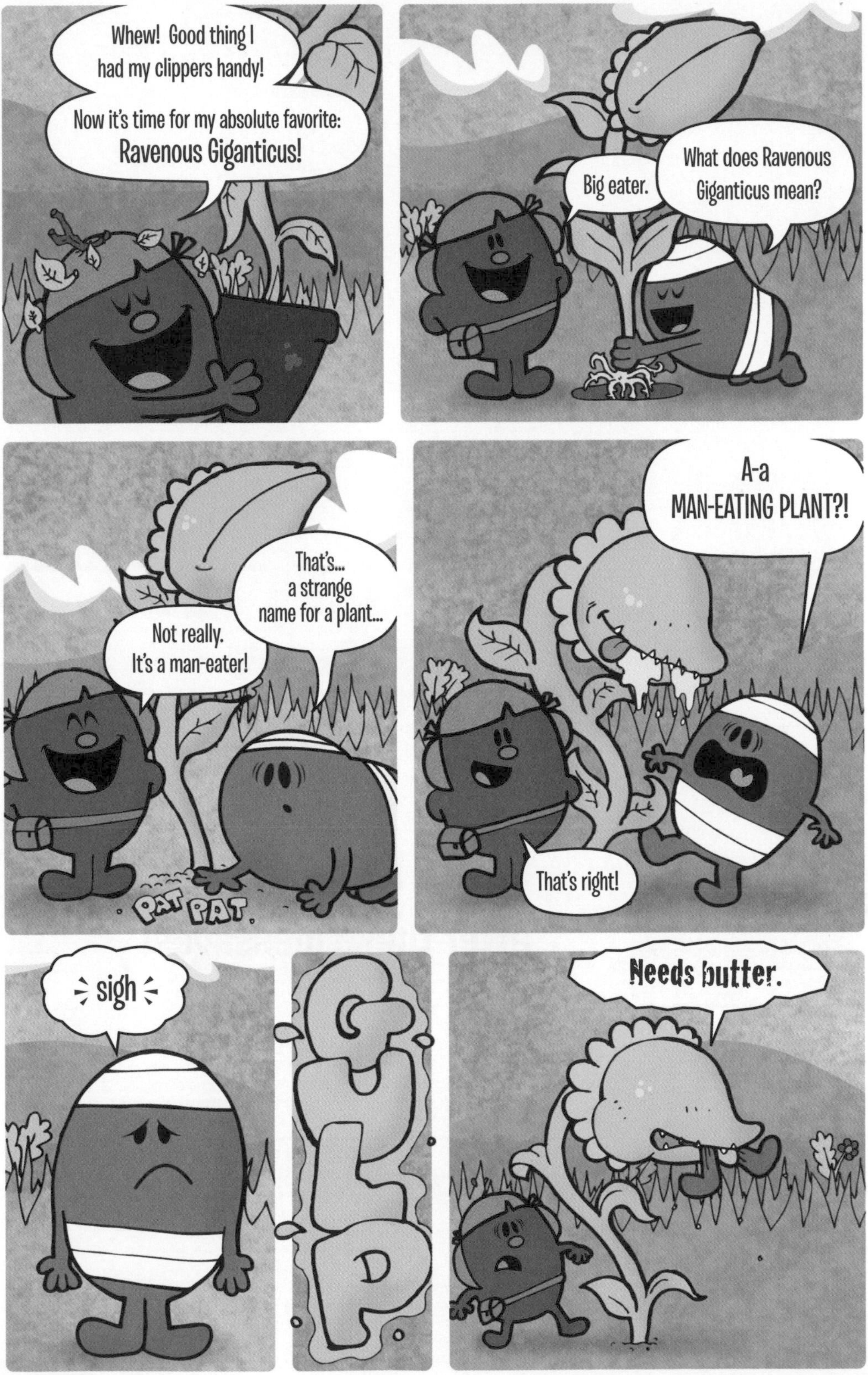
Whew! Good thing I had my clippers handy!
Now it's time for my absolute favorite: Ravenous Giganticus!
What does Ravenous Giganticus mean?
Big eater.
That's... a strange name for a plant...
Not really. It's a man-eater!
PAT PAT
A-a MAN-EATING PLANT?!
That's right!
sigh
GULP
Needs butter.

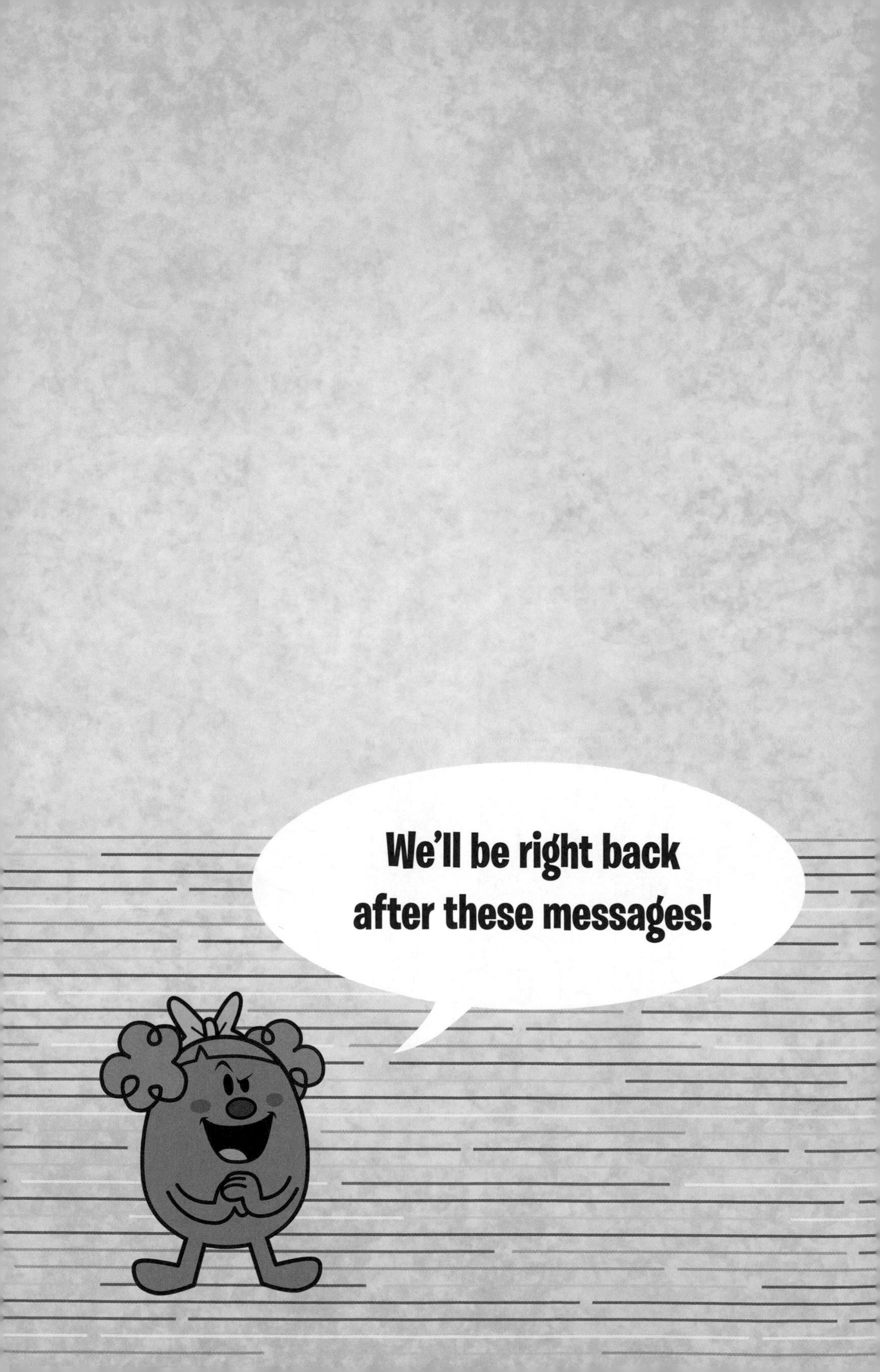
We'll be right back after these messages!

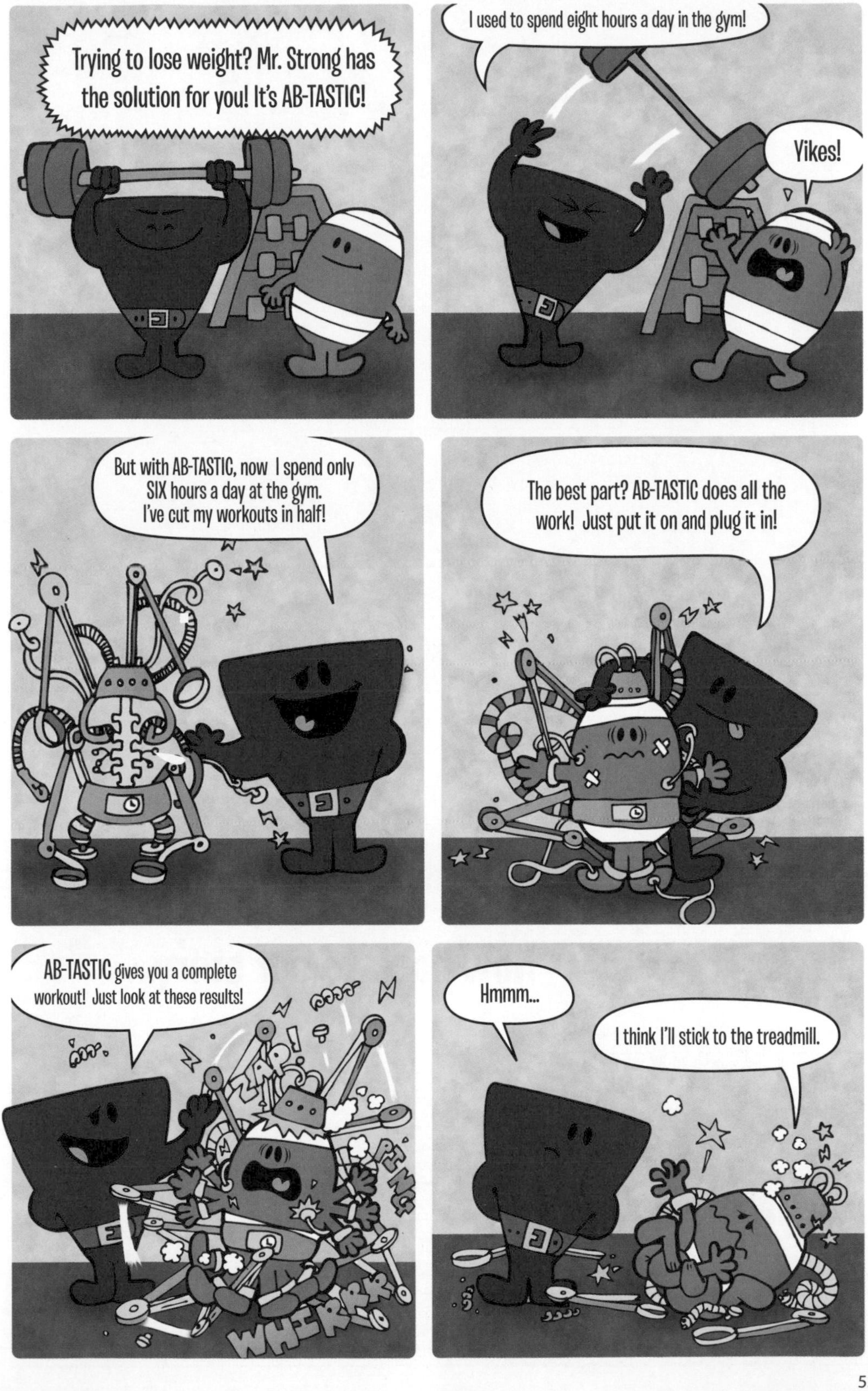
Trying to lose weight? Mr. Strong has the solution for you! It's AB-TASTIC!
I used to spend eight hours a day in the gym!
Yikes!
But with AB-TASTIC, now I spend only SIX hours a day at the gym. I've cut my workouts in half!
The best part? AB-TASTIC does all the work! Just put it on and plug it in!
AB-TASTIC gives you a complete workout! Just look at these results!
ZAP!
PING
WHIRRR
Hmmm...
I think I'll stick to the treadmill.

Now back to our story...

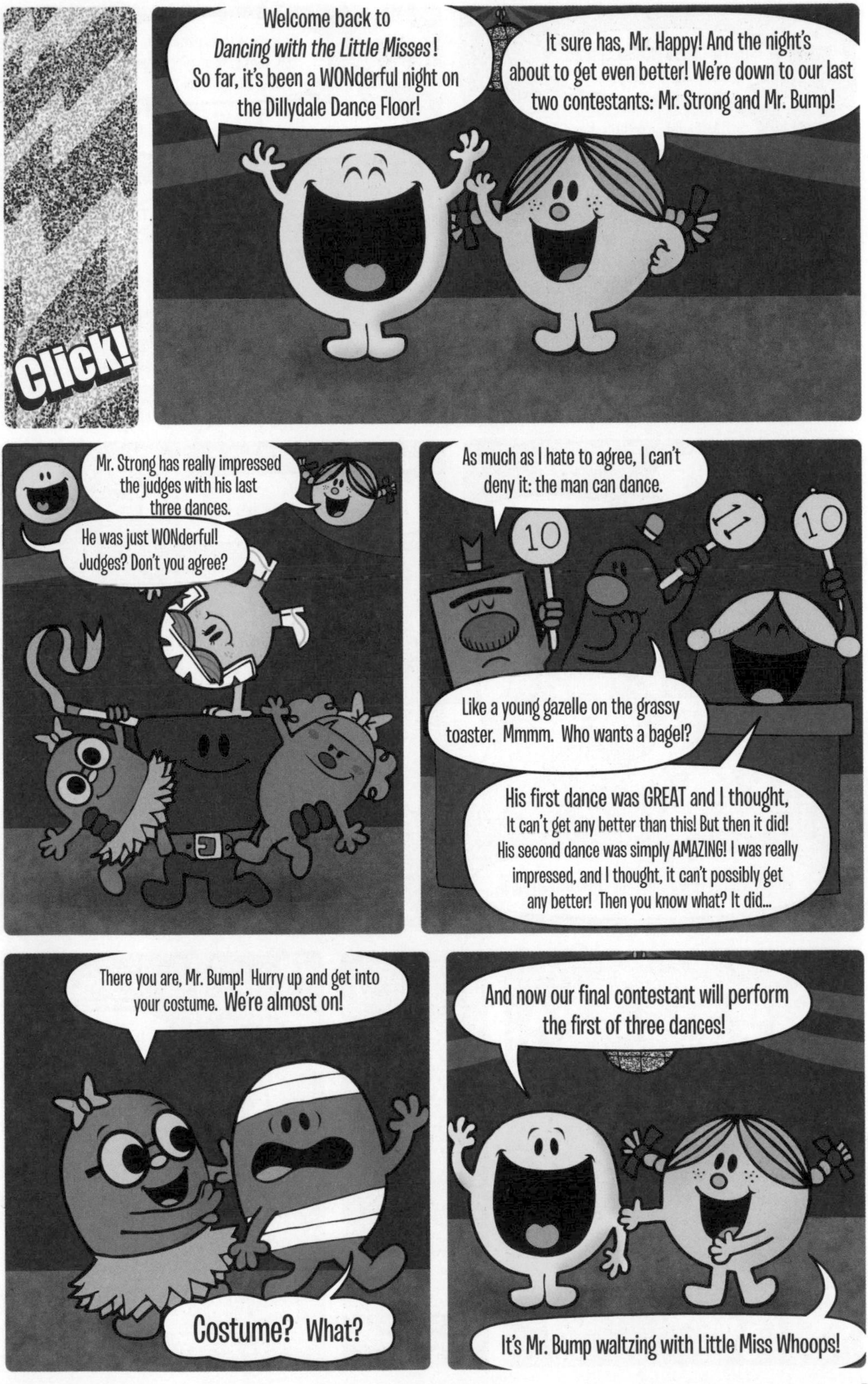

Click!
Welcome back to *Dancing with the Little Misses*! So far, it's been a WONderful night on the Dillydale Dance Floor!
It sure has, Mr. Happy! And the night's about to get even better! We're down to our last two contestants: Mr. Strong and Mr. Bump!
Mr. Strong has really impressed the judges with his last three dances.
He was just WONderful! Judges? Don't you agree?
As much as I hate to agree, I can't deny it: the man can dance.
10
11
10
Like a young gazelle on the grassy toaster. Mmmm. Who wants a bagel?
His first dance was GREAT and I thought, It can't get any better than this! But then it did! His second dance was simply AMAZING! I was really impressed, and I thought, it can't possibly get any better! Then you know what? It did...
There you are, Mr. Bump! Hurry up and get into your costume. We're almost on!
Costume? What?
And now our final contestant will perform the first of three dances!
It's Mr. Bump waltzing with Little Miss Whoops!

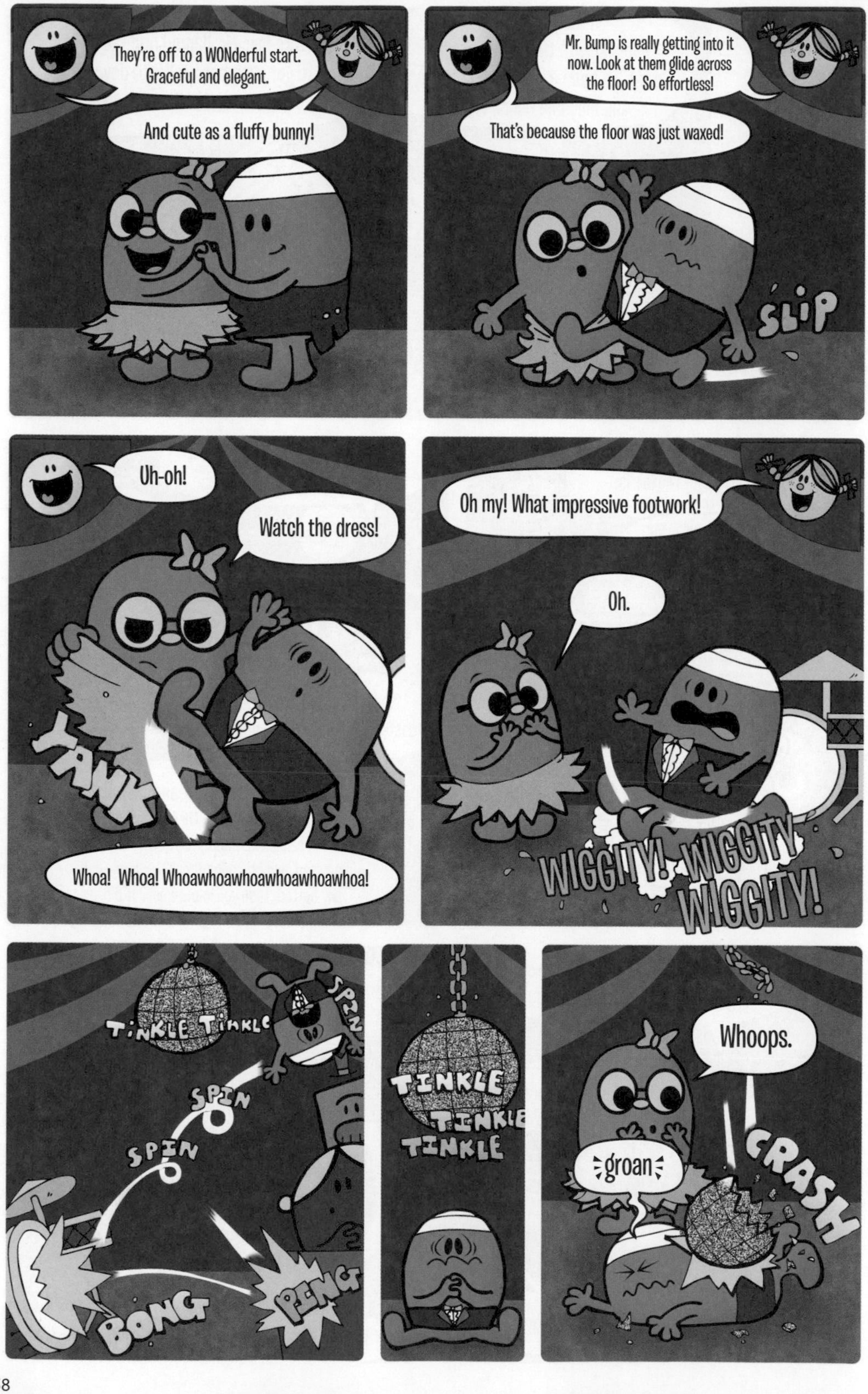
They're off to a WONderful start. Graceful and elegant.
And cute as a fluffy bunny!
Mr. Bump is really getting into it now. Look at them glide across the floor! So effortless!
That's because the floor was just waxed!
SLIP
Uh-oh!
Watch the dress!
YANK
Whoa! Whoa! Whoawhoawhoawhoawhoawhoa!
Oh my! What impressive footwork!
Oh.
WIGGITY! WIGGITY WIGGITY!
TINKLE TINKLE
SPIN
SPIN
SPIN
BONG
PENG
TINKLE
TINKLE
TINKLE
Whoops.
groan
CRASH

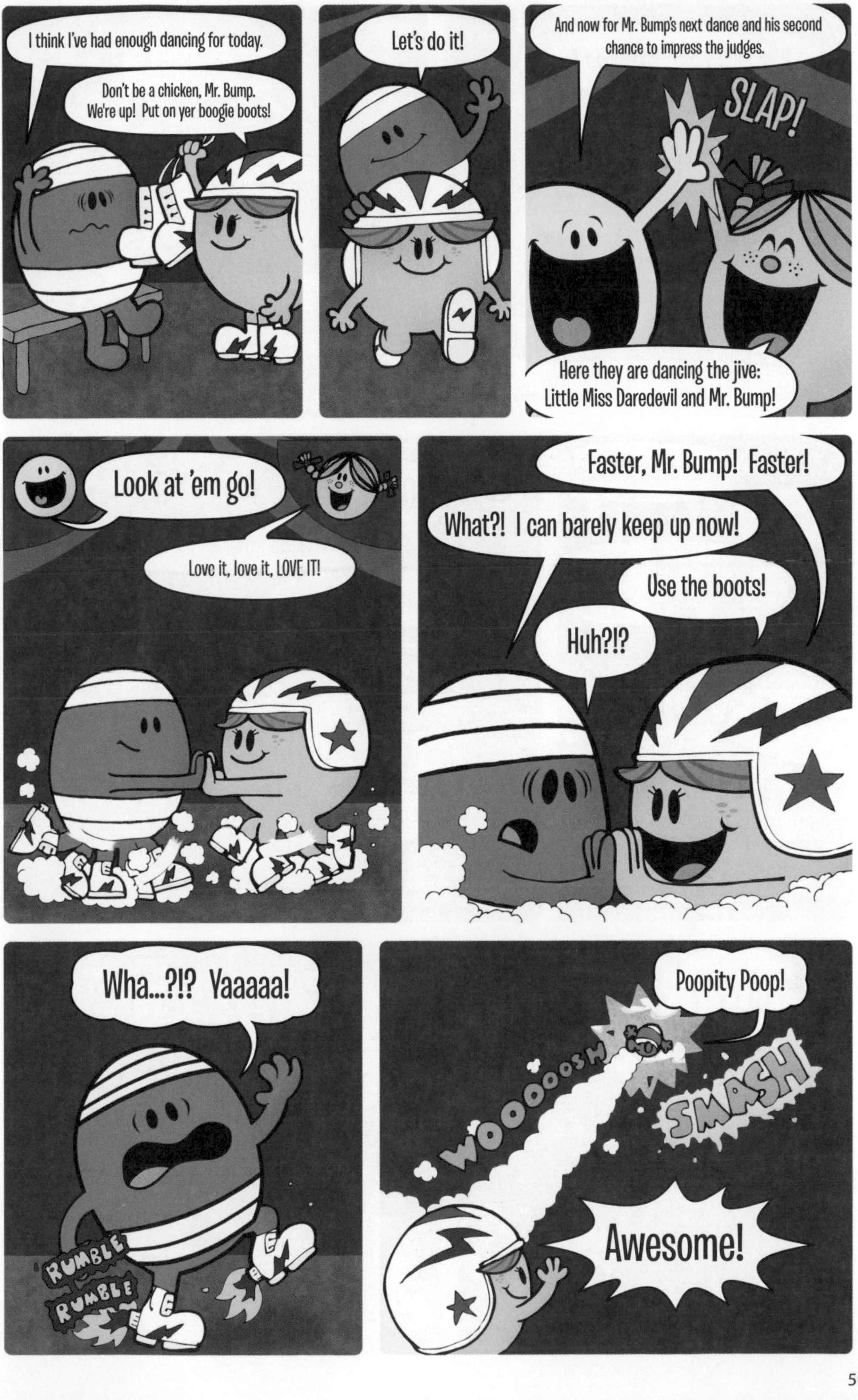

I think I've had enough dancing for today.
Don't be a chicken, Mr. Bump. We're up! Put on yer boogie boots!
Let's do it!
And now for Mr. Bump's next dance and his second chance to impress the judges.
SLAP!
Here they are dancing the jive: Little Miss Daredevil and Mr. Bump!
Look at 'em go!
Love it, love it, LOVE IT!
Faster, Mr. Bump! Faster!
What?! I can barely keep up now!
Use the boots!
Huh?!?
Wha...?!? Yaaaaa!
RUMBLE RUMBLE
Poopity Poop!
WOOOOOSH
SMASH
Awesome!

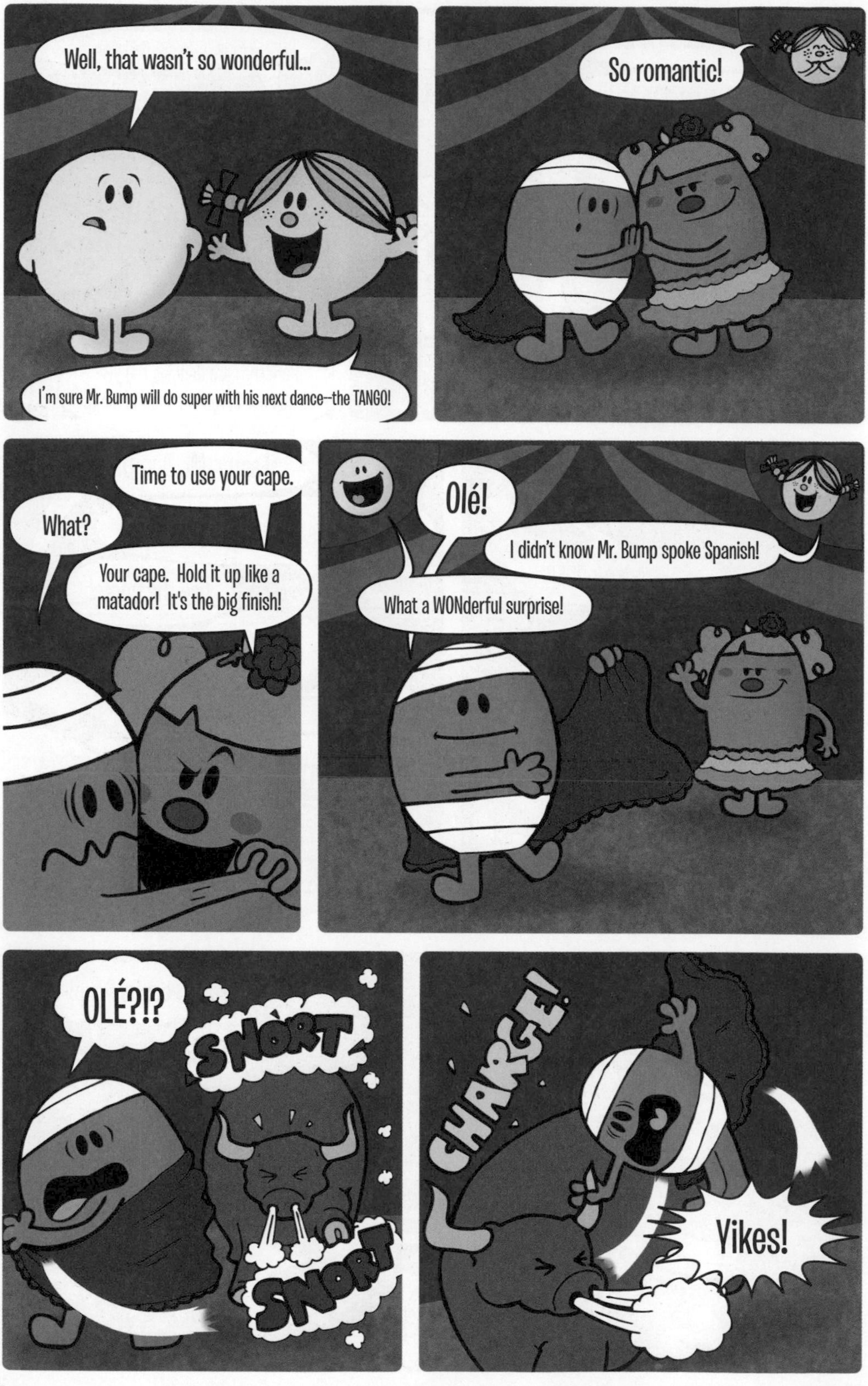
Well, that wasn't so wonderful...
I'm sure Mr. Bump will do super with his next dance—the TANGO!
So romantic!
Time to use your cape.
What?
Your cape. Hold it up like a matador! It's the big finish!
Olé!
I didn't know Mr. Bump spoke Spanish!
What a WONderful surprise!
OLÉ?!?
SNORT
SNORT
CHARGE!
Yikes!

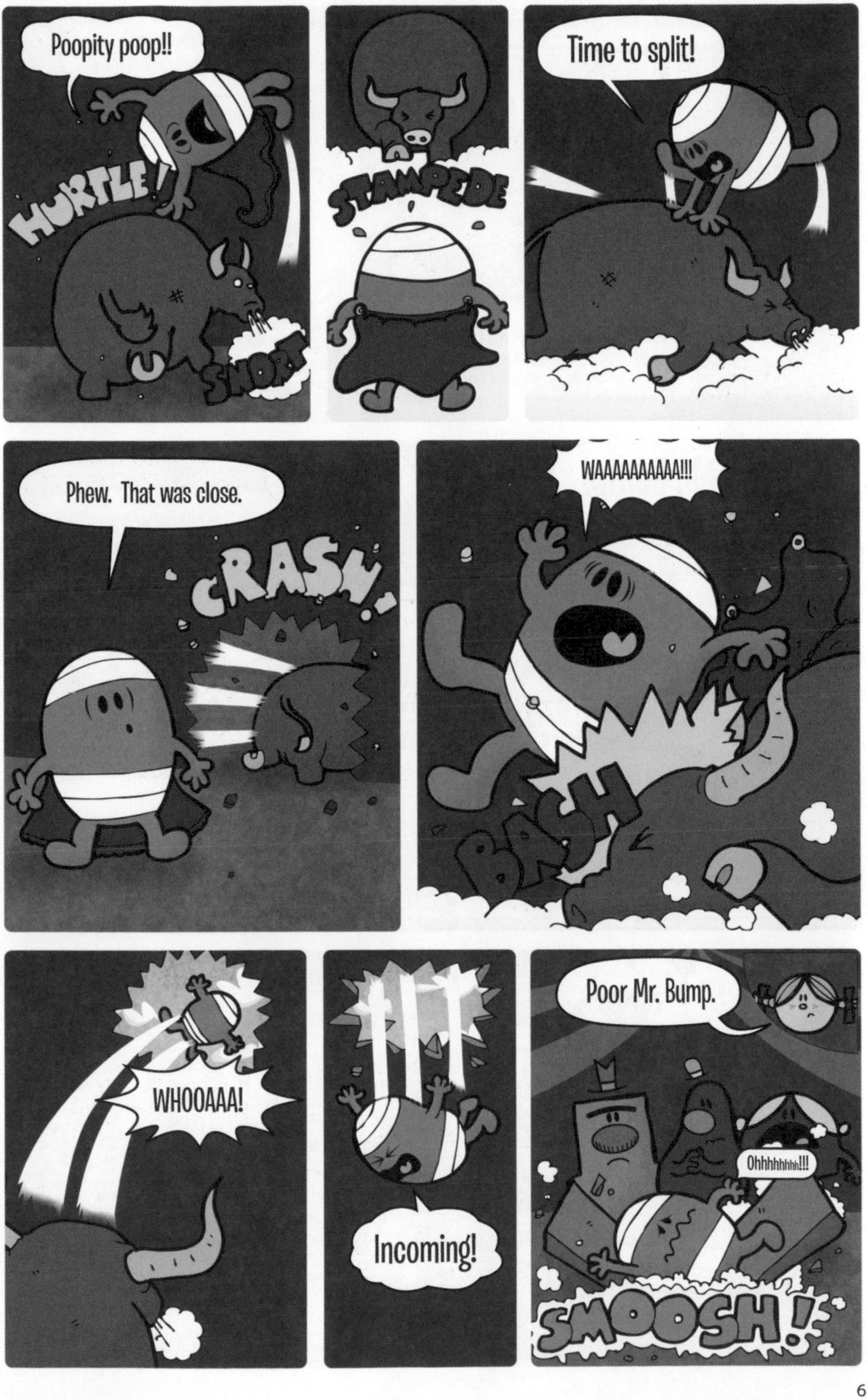
Poopity poop!!
HURTLE!
SNORT
STAMPEDE
Time to split!
Phew. That was close.
CRASH!
WAAAAAAAAAA!!!
BASH
WHOOAAA!
Incoming!
Poor Mr. Bump.
Ohhhhhhhh!!!
SMOOSH!

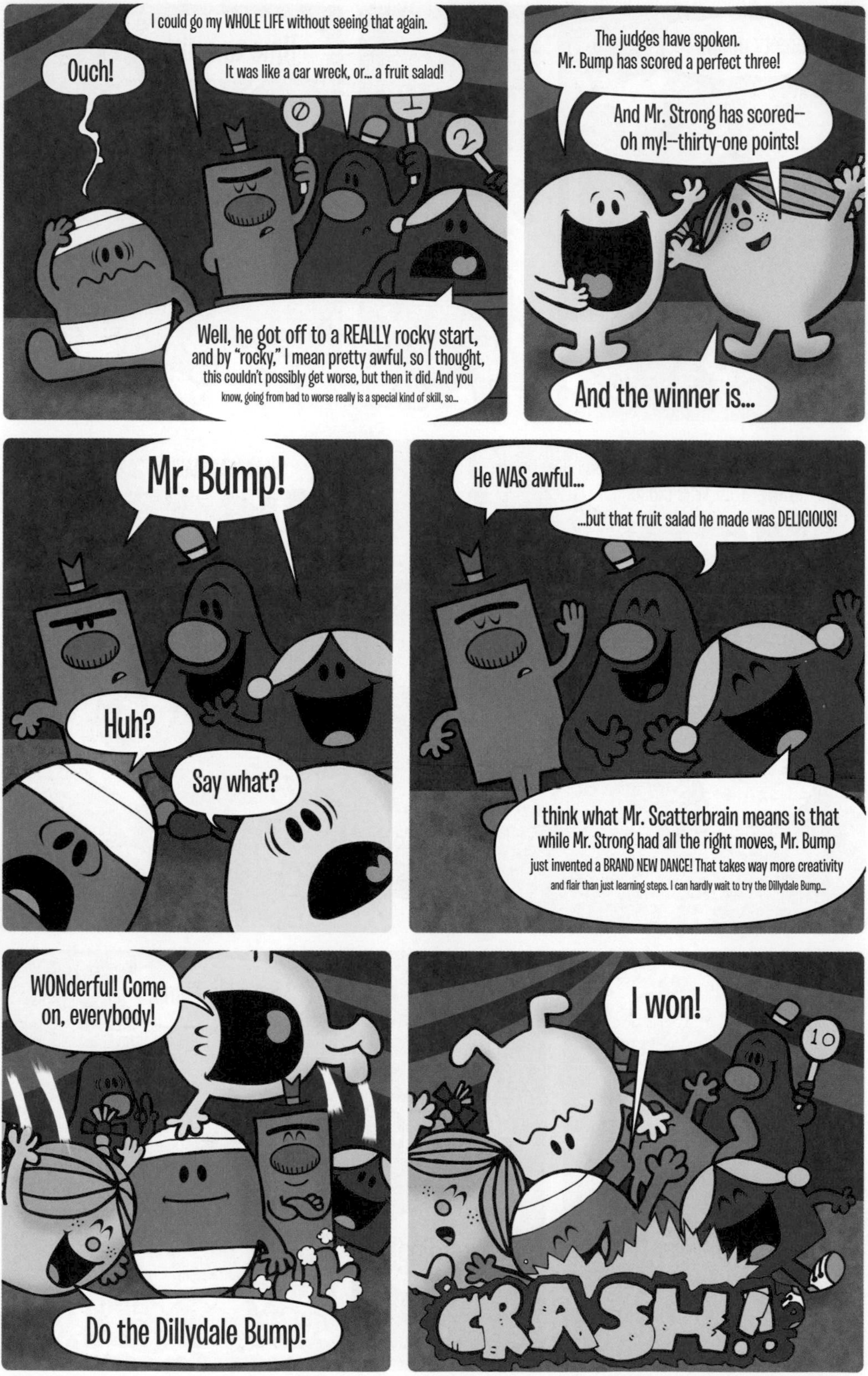
I could go my WHOLE LIFE without seeing that again.
Ouch!
It was like a car wreck, or... a fruit salad!
Well, he got off to a REALLY rocky start, and by "rocky," I mean pretty awful, so I thought, this couldn't possibly get worse, but then it did. And you know, going from bad to worse really is a special kind of skill, so...
The judges have spoken. Mr. Bump has scored a perfect three!
And Mr. Strong has scored–oh my!–thirty-one points!
And the winner is...
Mr. Bump!
Huh?
Say what?
He WAS awful...
...but that fruit salad he made was DELICIOUS!
I think what Mr. Scatterbrain means is that while Mr. Strong had all the right moves, Mr. Bump just invented a BRAND NEW DANCE! That takes way more creativity and flair than just learning steps. I can hardly wait to try the Dillydale Bump...
WONderful! Come on, everybody!
Do the Dillydale Bump!
I won!
CRASH!

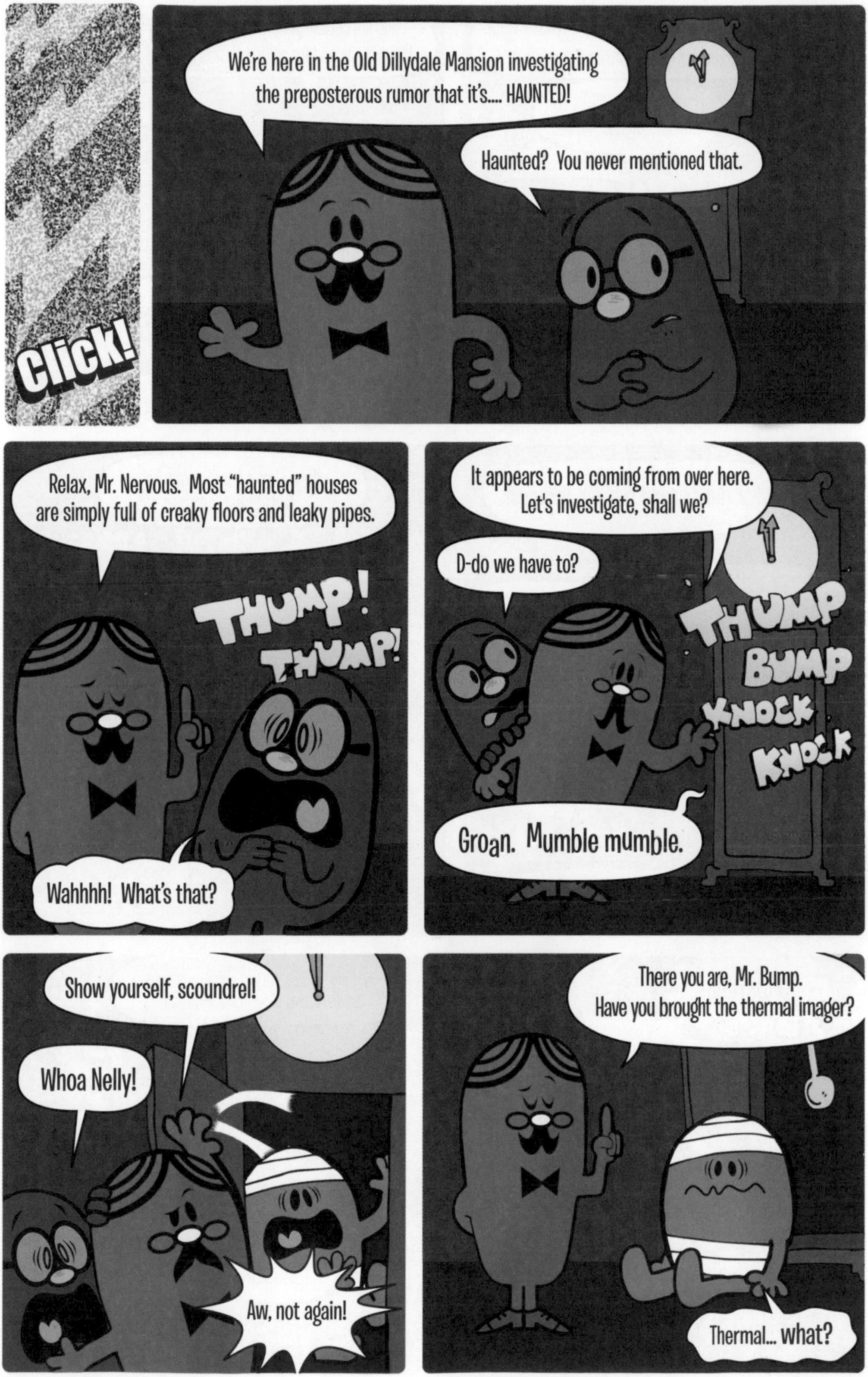
Click!
We're here in the Old Dillydale Mansion investigating the preposterous rumor that it's.... HAUNTED!
Haunted? You never mentioned that.
Relax, Mr. Nervous. Most "haunted" houses are simply full of creaky floors and leaky pipes.
THUMP! THUMP!
Wahhhh! What's that?
It appears to be coming from over here. Let's investigate, shall we?
D-do we have to?
THUMP BUMP KNOCK KNOCK
Groan. Mumble mumble.
Show yourself, scoundrel!
Whoa Nelly!
Aw, not again!
There you are, Mr. Bump. Have you brought the thermal imager?
Thermal... what?

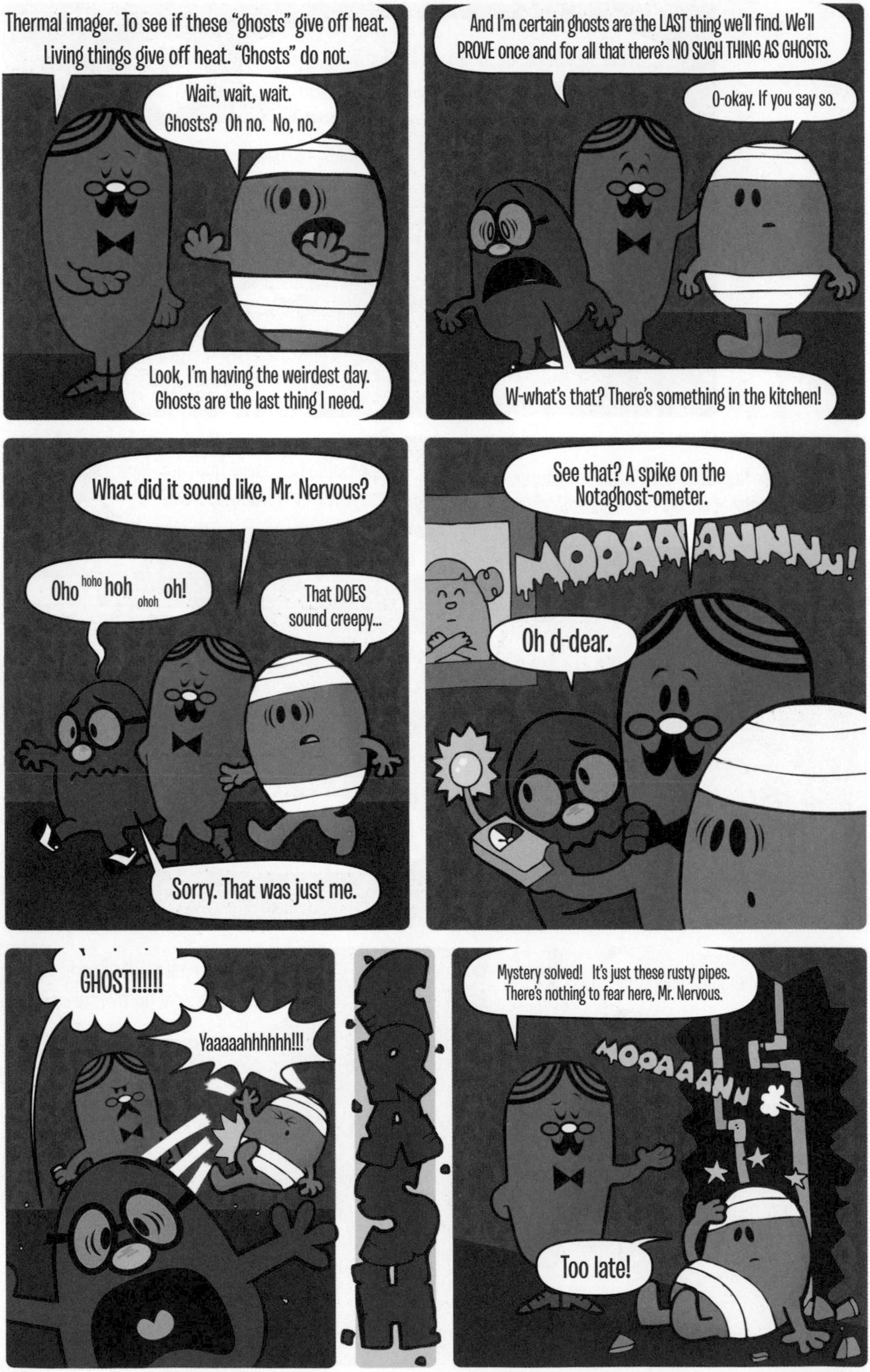
Thermal imager. To see if these "ghosts" give off heat. Living things give off heat. "Ghosts" do not.
Wait, wait, wait. Ghosts? Oh no. No, no.
Look, I'm having the weirdest day. Ghosts are the last thing I need.
And I'm certain ghosts are the LAST thing we'll find. We'll PROVE once and for all that there's NO SUCH THING AS GHOSTS.
O-okay. If you say so.
W-what's that? There's something in the kitchen!
What did it sound like, Mr. Nervous?
Oho hoho hoh ohoh oh!
That DOES sound creepy...
Sorry. That was just me.
See that? A spike on the Notaghost-ometer.
Oh d-dear.
GHOST!!!!!!
Yaaaaahhhhhh!!!
CRASH
Mystery solved! It's just these rusty pipes. There's nothing to fear here, Mr. Nervous.
MOOAAANN
Too late!

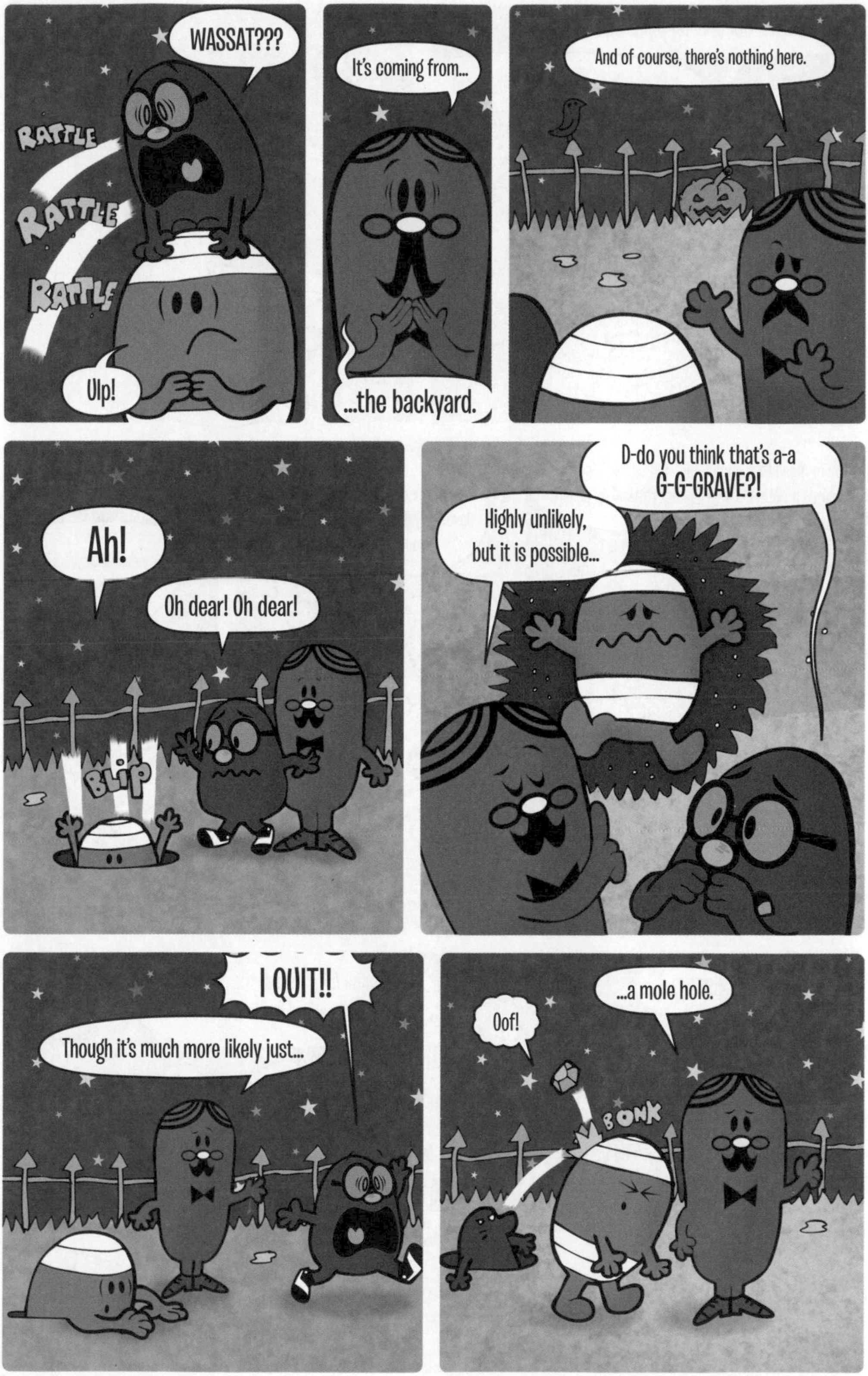
WASSAT???
RATTLE
RATTLE
RATTLE
Ulp!
It's coming from...
...the backyard.
And of course, there's nothing here.
Ah!
Oh dear! Oh dear!
BLIP
D-do you think that's a-a G-G-GRAVE?!
Highly unlikely, but it is possible...
I QUIT!!
Though it's much more likely just...
...a mole hole.
Oof!
BONK

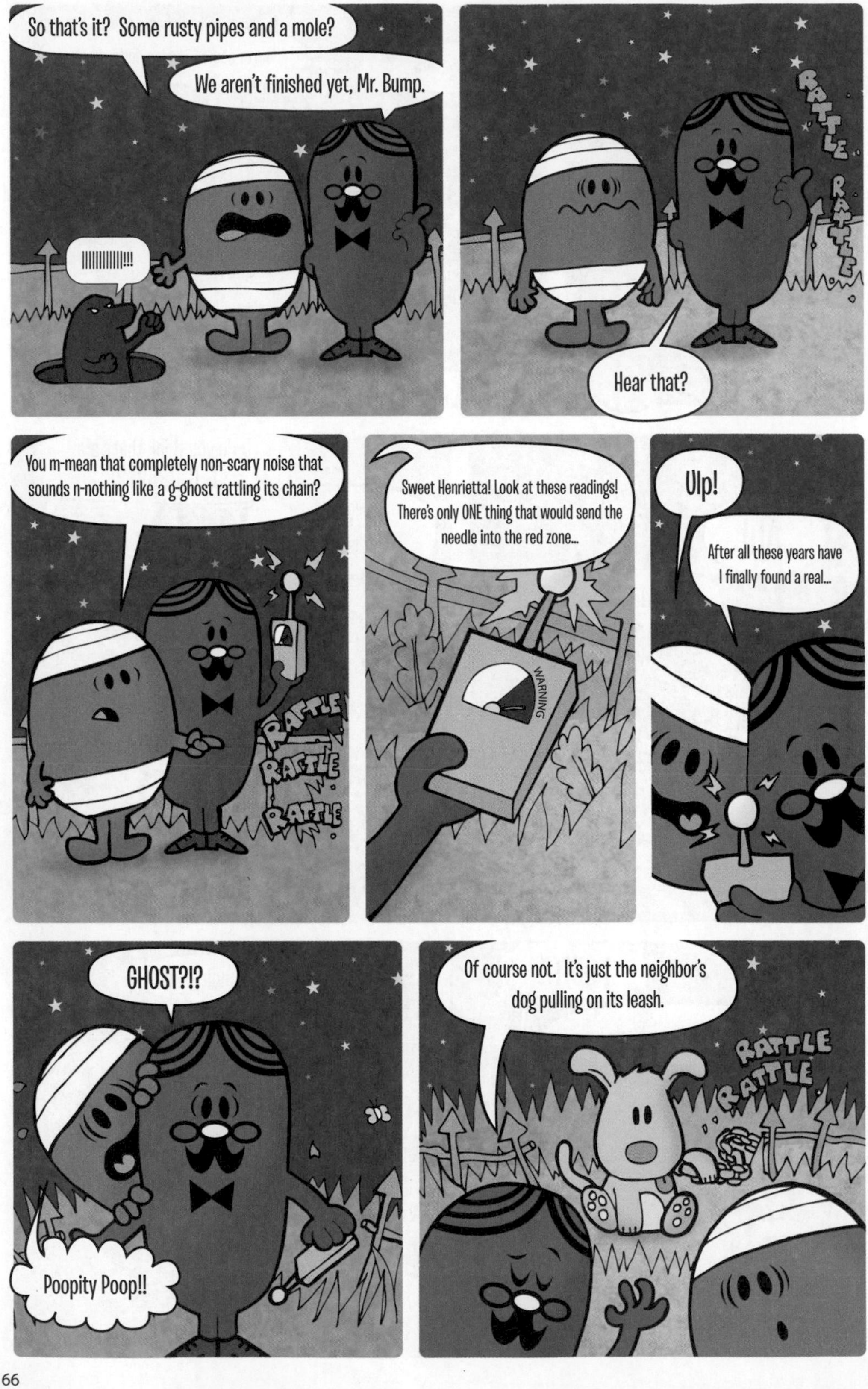

So that's it? Some rusty pipes and a mole?
We aren't finished yet, Mr. Bump.
!!!!!!!!!!!!!!!
RATTLE
RATTLE
Hear that?
You m-mean that completely non-scary noise that sounds n-nothing like a g-ghost rattling its chain?
RATTLE
RATTLE
RATTLE
Sweet Henrietta! Look at these readings! There's only ONE thing that would send the needle into the red zone...
WARNING
Ulp!
After all these years have I finally found a real...
GHOST?!?
Poopity Poop!!
Of course not. It's just the neighbor's dog pulling on its leash.
RATTLE
RATTLE

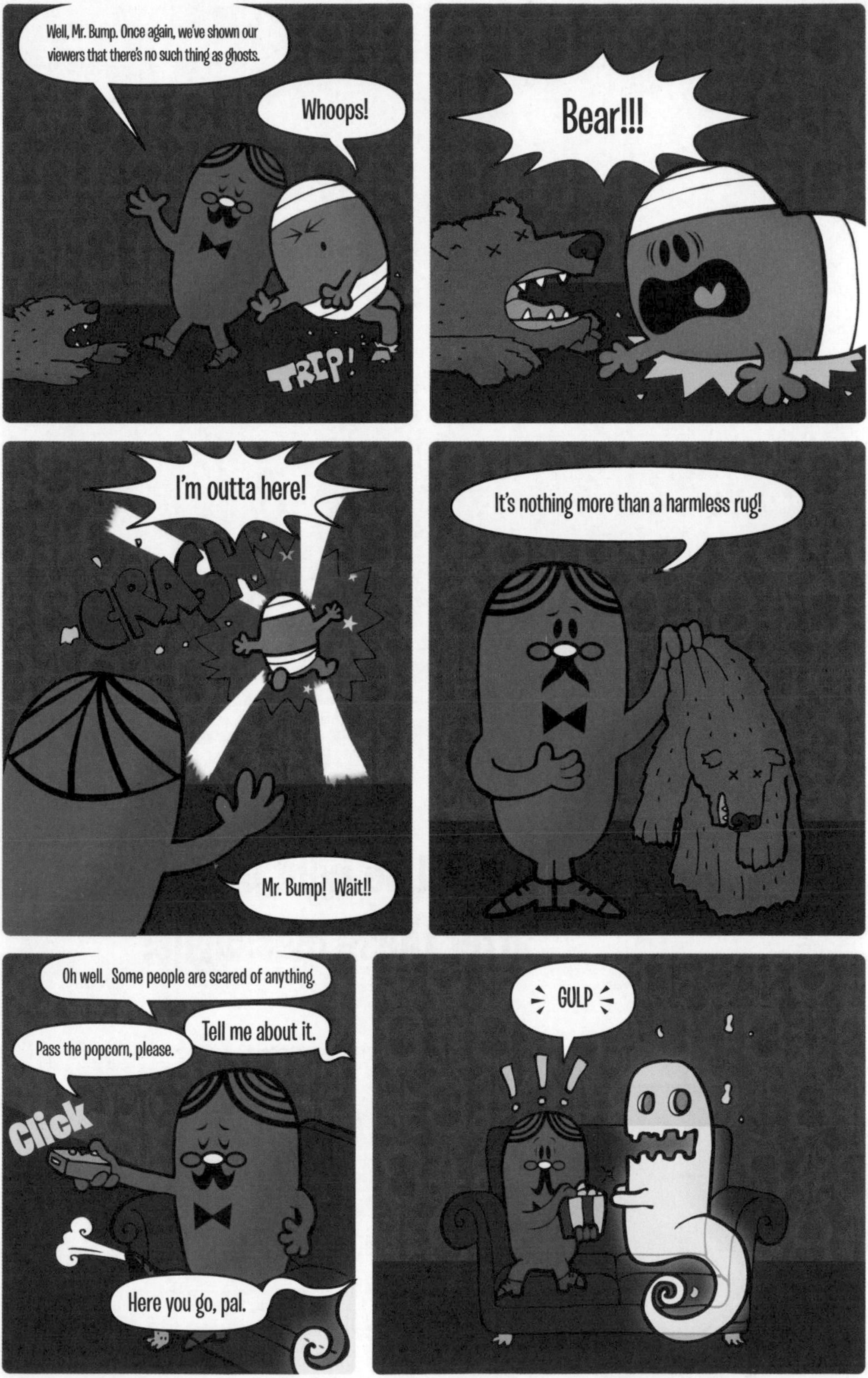
Well, Mr. Bump. Once again, we've shown our viewers that there's no such thing as ghosts.
Whoops!
TRIP!
Bear!!!
I'm outta here!
CRASH
Mr. Bump! Wait!!
It's nothing more than a harmless rug!
Oh well. Some people are scared of anything.
Tell me about it.
Pass the popcorn, please.
Click
Here you go, pal.
GULP

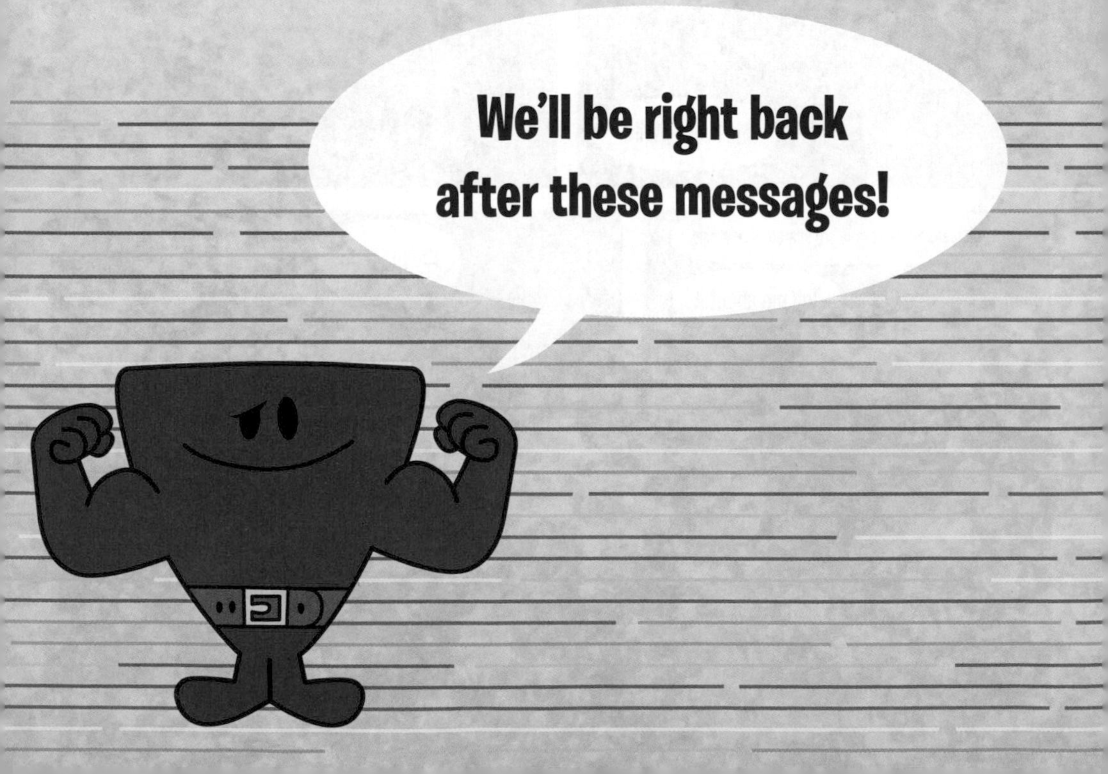
We'll be right back after these messages!

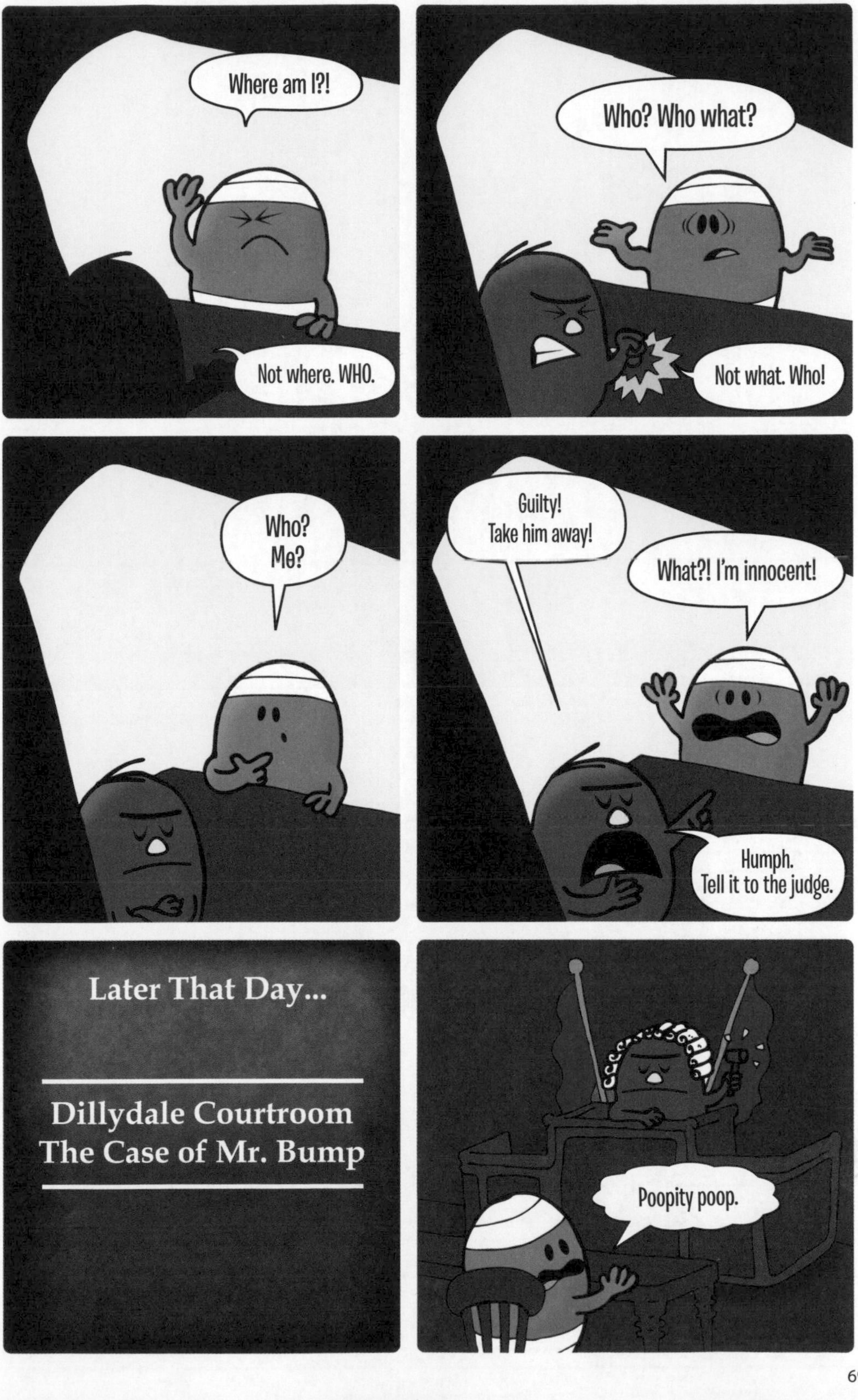
Where am I?!
Not where. WHO.
Who? Who what?
Not what. Who!
Who? Me?
Guilty! Take him away!
What?! I'm innocent!
Humph. Tell it to the judge.
Later That Day...
Dillydale Courtroom
The Case of Mr. Bump
Poopity poop.

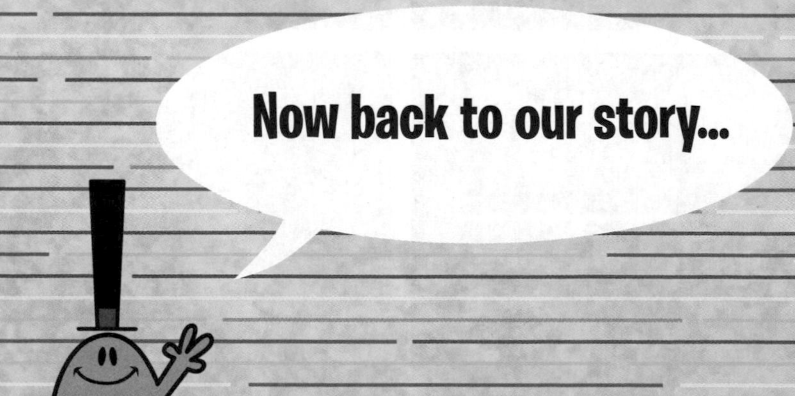
Now back to our story...

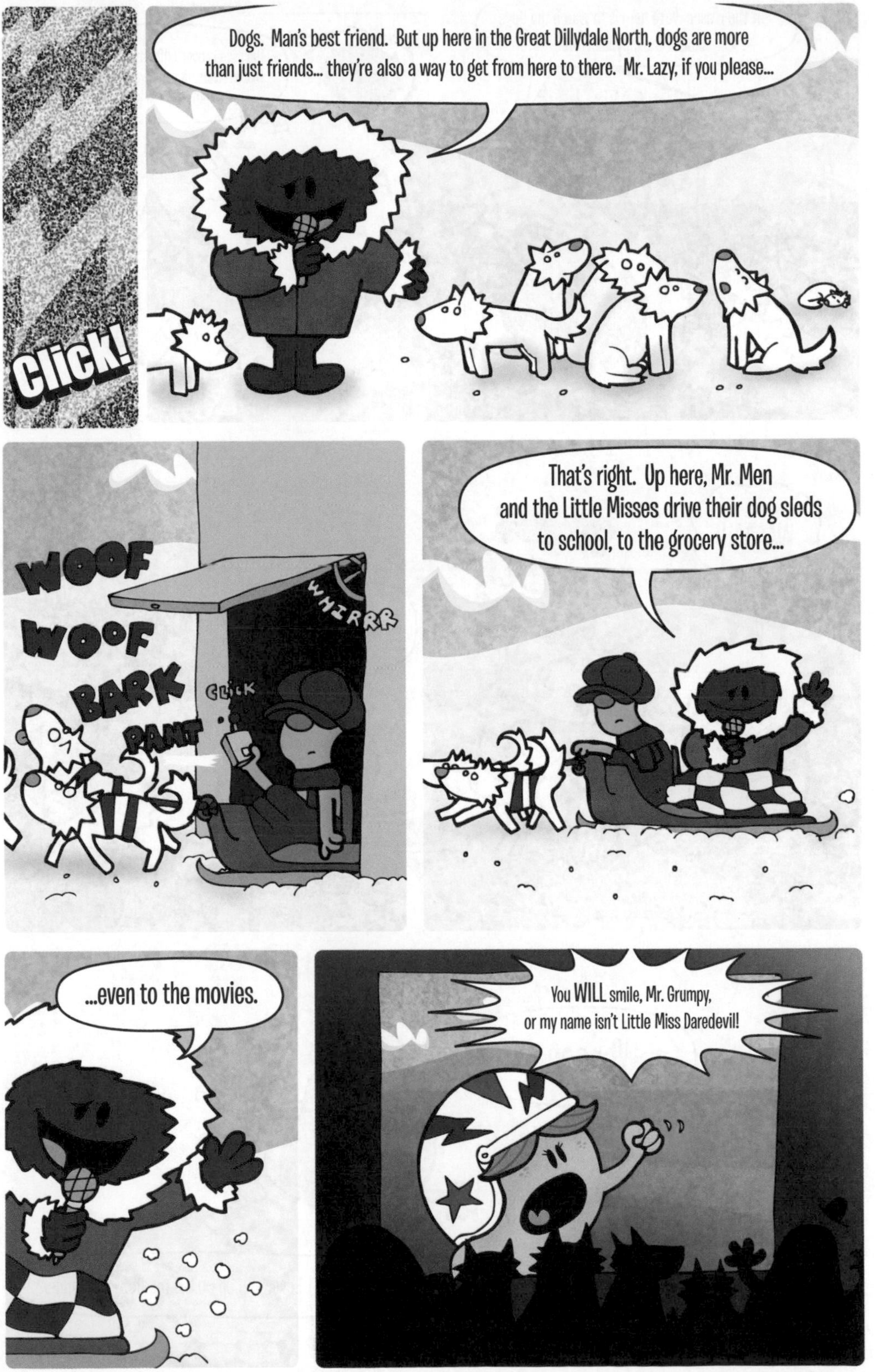

Dogs. Man's best friend. But up here in the Great Dillydale North, dogs are more than just friends... they're also a way to get from here to there. Mr. Lazy, if you please...
Click!
WOOF
WOOF
BARK
PANT
CLICK
WHIRRR
That's right. Up here, Mr. Men and the Little Misses drive their dog sleds to school, to the grocery store...
...even to the movies.
You WILL smile, Mr. Grumpy, or my name isn't Little Miss Daredevil!

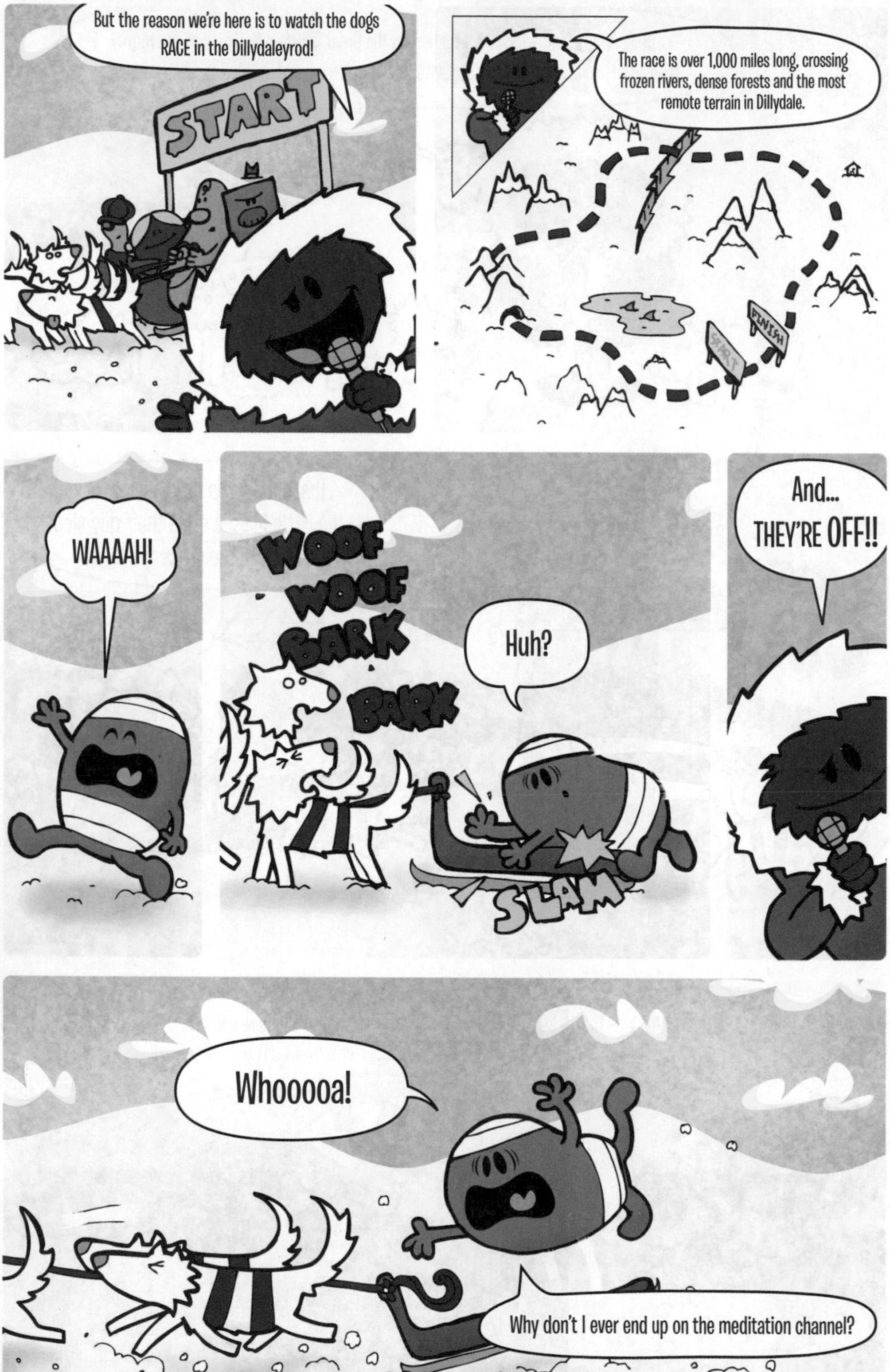
But the reason we're here is to watch the dogs RACE in the Dillydaleyrod!
START
The race is over 1,000 miles long, crossing frozen rivers, dense forests and the most remote terrain in Dillydale.
FINISH
START
WAAAAH!
WOOF
WOOF
BARK
BARK
Huh?
SLAM
And...
THEY'RE OFF!!
Whoooa!
Why don't I ever end up on the meditation channel?

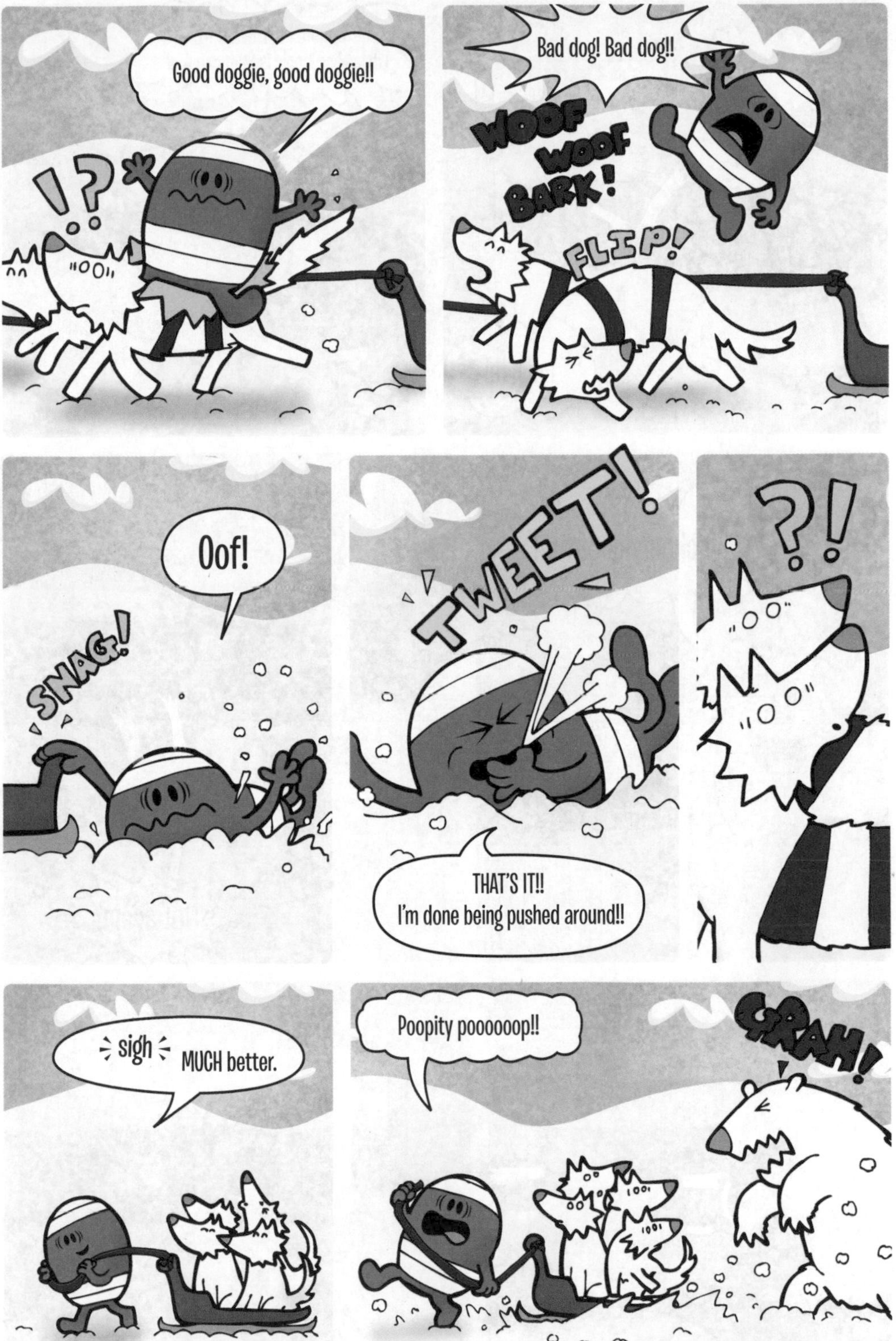
Good doggie, good doggie!!
!?
Bad dog! Bad dog!!
WOOF
WOOF
BARK!
FLIP!
SNAG!
Oof!
TWEET!
THAT'S IT!!
I'm done being pushed around!!
?!
sigh MUCH better.
Poopity poooooop!!
GRAH!

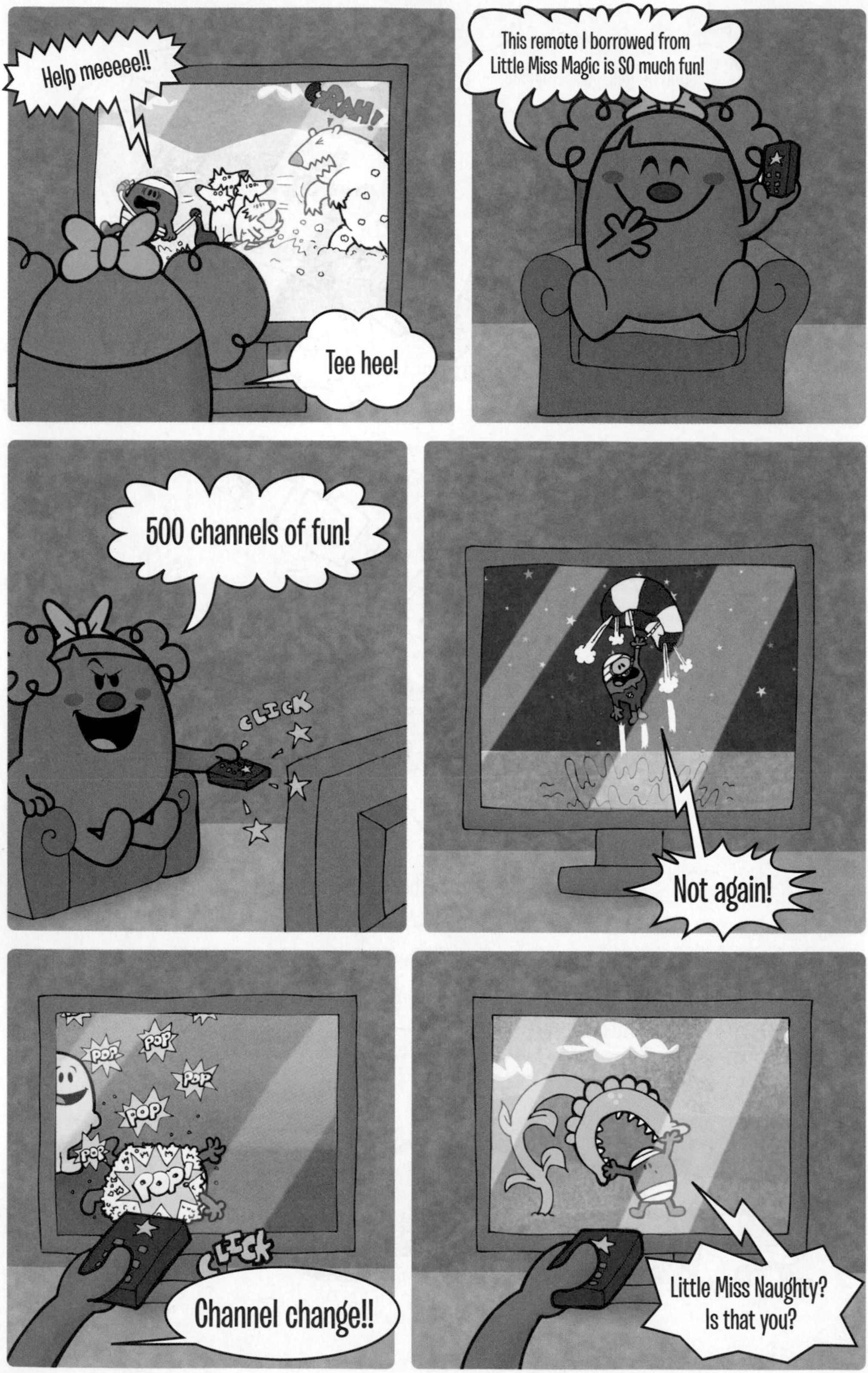
Help meeeee!!
Tee hee!
This remote I borrowed from Little Miss Magic is SO much fun!
500 channels of fun!
CLICK
Not again!
POP
POP
POP
POP
POP
POP!
CLICK
Channel change!!
Little Miss Naughty? Is that you?

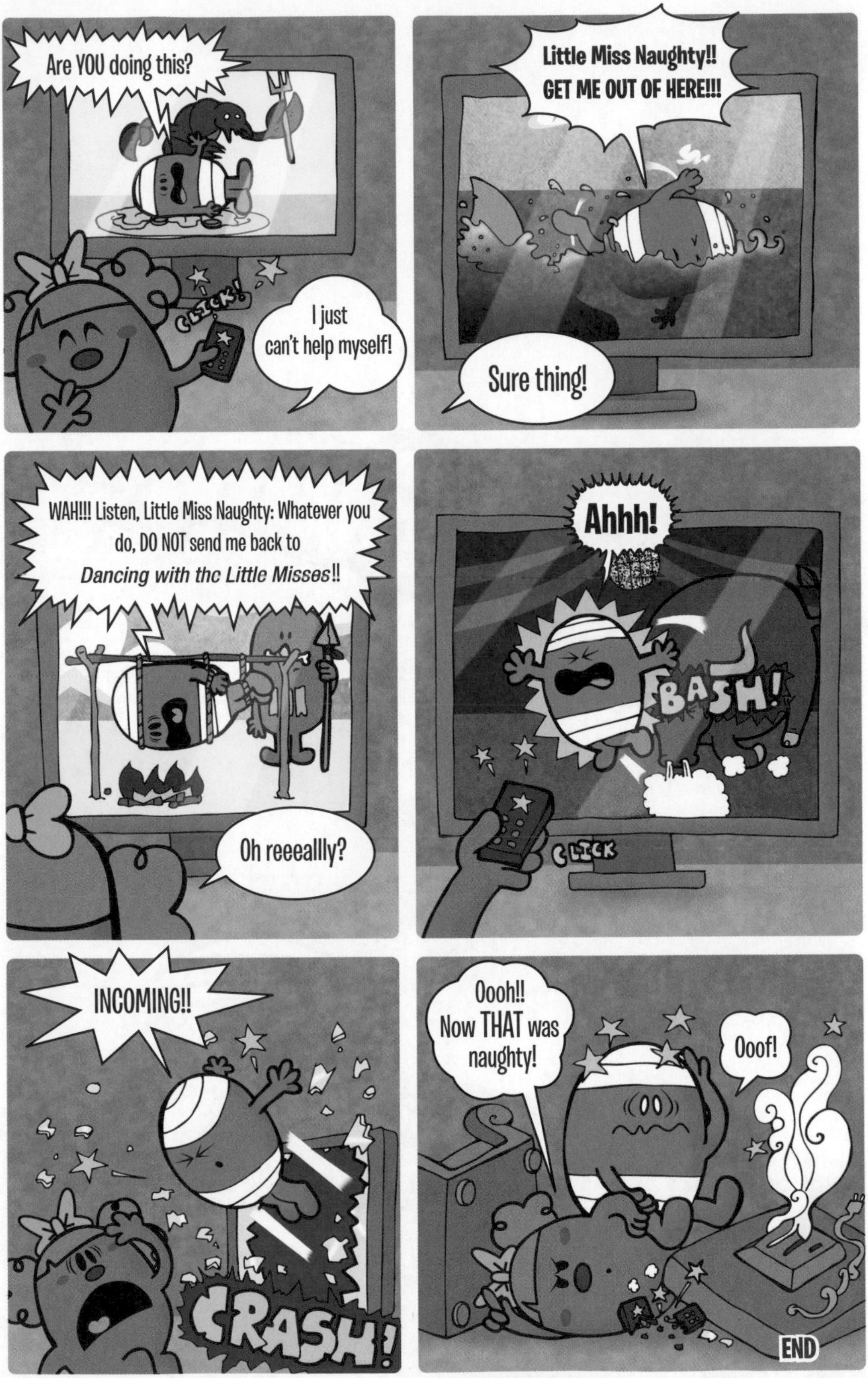
Are YOU doing this?
CLICK!
I just can't help myself!
Little Miss Naughty!! GET ME OUT OF HERE!!!
Sure thing!
WAH!!! Listen, Little Miss Naughty: Whatever you do, DO NOT send me back to *Dancing with the Little Misses*!!
Oh reeeallly?
Ahhh!
BASH!
CLICK
INCOMING!!
CRASH!
Oooh!! Now THAT was naughty!
Ooof!
END

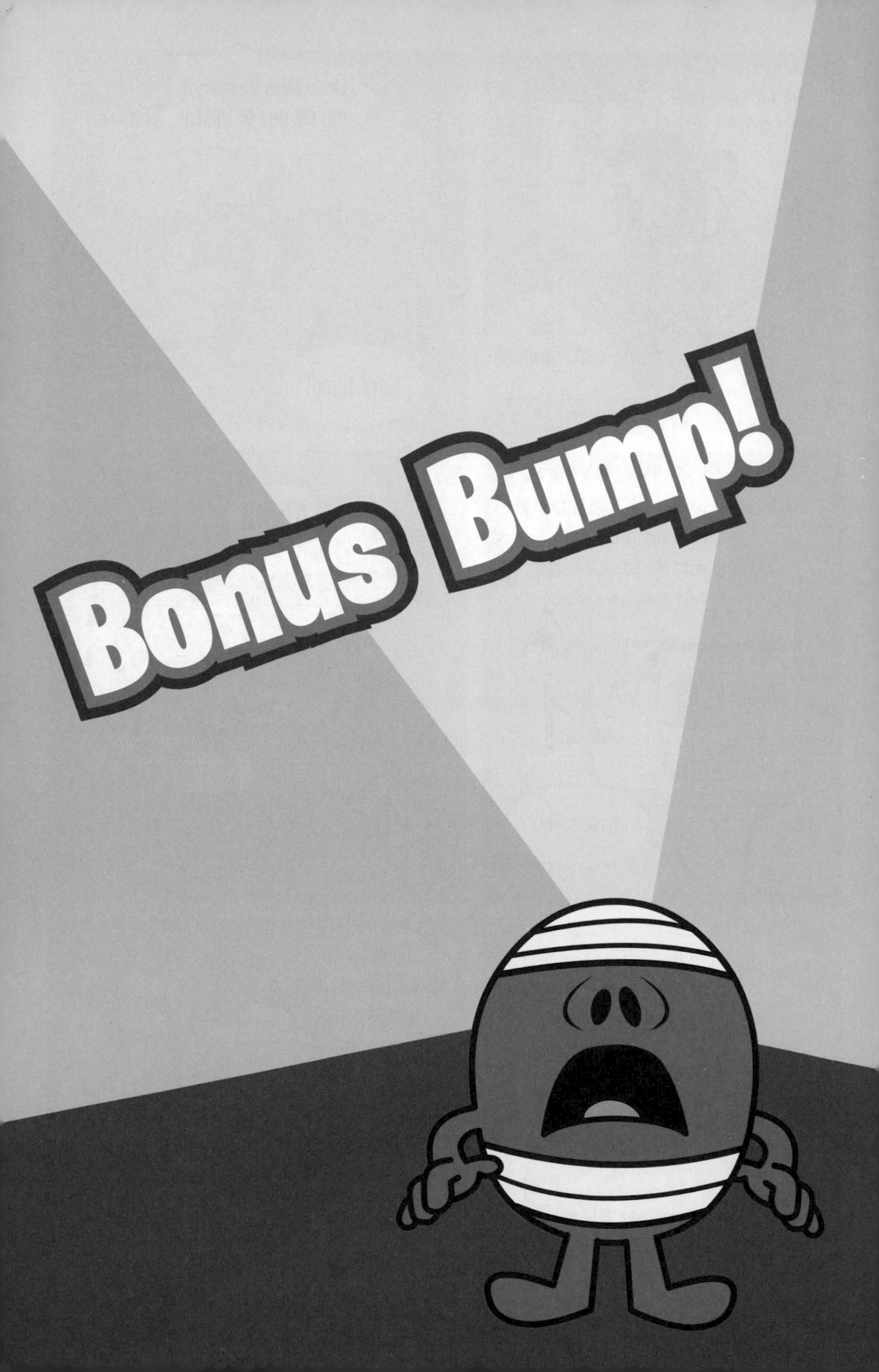
Bonus Bump!

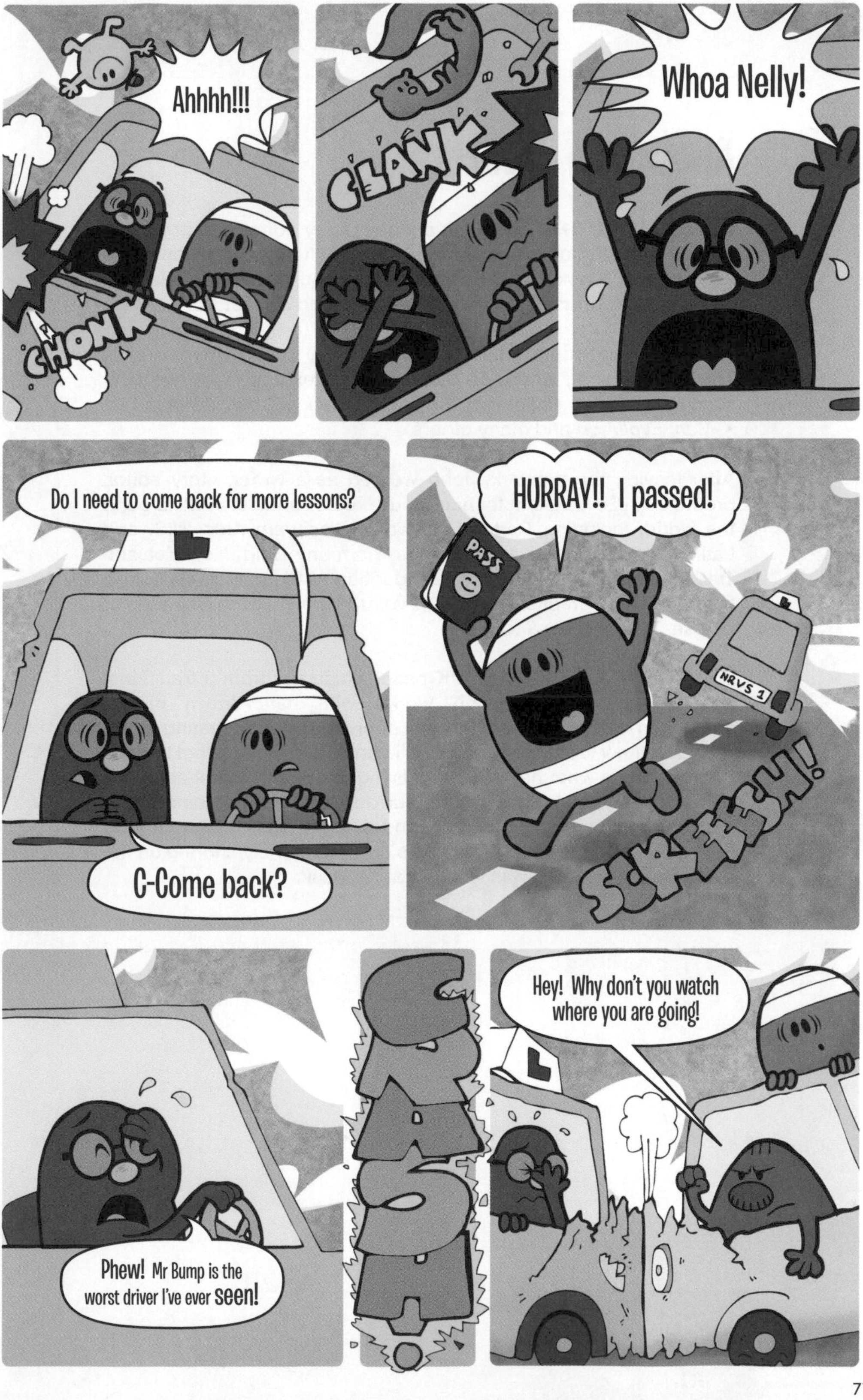
Ahhhh!!!
CHONK
CLANK
Whoa Nelly!
Do I need to come back for more lessons?
C-Come back?
HURRAY!! I passed!
PASS
NRVS 1
SCREEECH!
Phew! Mr Bump is the worst driver I've ever seen!
Hey! Why don't you watch where you are going!

About the Creators

John Hardman has been a writer, story editor and producer, as well as a studio and network executive. His career began as an executive at Klasky Csupo Studios, working on such acclaimed projects as *Rugrats*, *The Wild Thornberrys* and *Rocket Power*.

John had tremendous success at Kids' WB!, the children's arm of The WB Network, where he worked as an executive on the very successful series *Pokémon*, *Yu-Gi-Oh!*, *Jackie Chan Adventures*, *X-Men: Evolution* and many others.

After leaving the network, John worked as a writer, story editor, producer and consultant for numerous studios and networks around the world, including Cartoon Network, Discovery Kids (U.S. and Latin America), American Greetings, Harmony Gold, New Zealand Trade & Enterprise, Mike Young Productions and many more. John's favorite writing credits include *Maryoku Yummy*, *Zatch Bell* and, of course, *The Mr. Men Show*.

Matthew Britton is a UK-based illustrator from a traditional fine arts background, who works with hand-drawn media, converting it into digital artwork full of energy and interesting twisty lines. Matthew loves his job, and still can't quite believe that he gets to draw, doing what he loves for a living! He works out of an 1870s house in the Welsh countryside, surrounded by mountains and a beautiful national park, his wife, and a large black Labrador who lives a life of luxury and dog biscuits and is generally snoring on the sofa whenever Matthew is working at his desk.